MW01616180

The Amulet

Journey to Sirok

The Elias Chronicles~Book I

Also by E.G. Kardos

Zen Master Next Door

Coming soon:

The Elias Chronicles~Book II

Journey Beneath Sirok

For Zach, Stephanie

Mary and Elizabeth

May your heart forever be your guide.

"A hero ventures forth from the world of common day into a region of supernatural wonder. Fabulous forces are there encountered and a decisive victory is won."

Joseph Campbell

Acknowledgements

Writing is a solitary journey. Getting from the first step to the last, however, takes many champions along the way. Many helped me up on my feet when I stumbled, some showed me the best turn in the road when I searched aimlessly, at times, some encouraged me to keep going even when the path I took seemed to lead to a dead-end.

My good friend and author, Roy Dimond, helped me with many aspects of my journey, and I owe him a great debt of gratitude.

Bestselling author Dean King has always made time to help me ever since the day I met him a decade and a half ago. I hope this story makes him proud.

My thanks go to Dr. Leila Christenbury for being an early reader and giving me a "thumbs up."

Thank you to C.S. Marks, author, who freely pointed me in the right direction and shared her many experiences with me.

Thank you Mom and Dad. Without them, this tale would never have been told.

My children, Zach, Stephanie, Mary and Elizabeth are the reason I write. They inspire me with their endless imagination and zest for life. They may not know it, but they are with me every day.

Last, I want to thank Kristin, my wife of more than thirty years, for her enduring love and friendship.

ONE
Legend

"When the serpent is slithering inside, you will know it, but only with the gift will you understand how it lives and how it dies."

That's where she always began.

Like many women before her, Nattymama passed down a legend to all who would listen. There were those, of course, who would hear but would not heed her words. Others listened and they would find their rewards.

On the spring equinox at the precise time that winter turned to spring, Nattymama dusted off a tattered scroll and read aloud to the children in the center of the village. Her account began where the castle now lay in ruins to the north of the village on a small rocky mountain. She told her tale as if it happened only yesterday—or for that matter, might just happen again. Her story was known to many as *The Legend of Sirok.*

As a young boy, Elias sat front and center and listened to Nattymama, his grandmother, bring to life the events she traced back a thousand years. He hung on to her every word. Getting through the scary scenes took all the bravery he could muster. Keeping one eye closed during some scenes, he patiently waited for his favorite parts. He couldn't get enough of the battle scene as well as how the story ended. For many years to come, he would hear her voice in his head just as if he was listening to her story for the first time. Oftentimes he thought of the legend's conclusion and its meaning.

"Centuries ago," Nattymama said, ending the story as she looked out to the faces around her, "a lightning bolt hurtled upward from the center of the Castle of Sirok. The beam split the clear sky. It was then that the thunder rumbled like a stampede of a thousand water buffalo as bloated clouds the color of dried ox blood gobbled up the open sky. All was dark—motionless. One moment passed and then another, but on the third tick of a clock, sheets of rain began to pelt the kingdom. This wasn't like most storms. Moments later, it was clear the downpour had washed away what contaminated the gilded kingdom.

Not long after the rainstorm, curls of black smoke billowed from somewhere near the core of Sirok. The huge flames cast an eerie glow on the naked kingdom. Hours passed and the flames subsided. Still masked by smoke, the sun eventually shone through misshapen holes in the black blanket. With little warning, what was left of the suffocating smoke vanished, letting more threads of light reveal the stone structures high on the mountaintop. Without so much as a smoldering ember, Sirok was reborn.

A bird sang followed by another. The water was clean and the air was fresh. The buildings were bright and the roads led freely in and out. The people saw each other in a new way and smiled.

Filled with joy, the warrior mounted a horse and rode down the rocky path that few dared to travel. At the foot of the mountain, a hundred or so villagers looked on like zombies. They said little as they witnessed such chaos only minutes earlier turn into something new—something altogether different from what had stood before.

As the young man grew visibly larger to the masses, the only sounds one could hear were the pounding of the hooves drubbing on the rocky soil. *Thump, thump, thump!* The warrior raced up to where the people gathered and yanked on the reins much to the displeasure of his faithful steed.

'What the evil one seized, the people of the kingdom have reclaimed. With this newfound will, we are now free and have washed our hands of our needless guilt. We have nothing to fear as we know who we are.'

The people before the warrior were a field of statues who said nothing, much to his surprise.

'Don't you see? Our misguided ways had become a way of life. We believed in the wrong things but it is a new day for us—and you— as we are the victors.'

'So where is he? *The evil one?*' a man shouted from the crowd.

'He is victim of his own undoing and sealed his fate in the eternal fire of his own making,' said the warrior. 'Our resolve is golden.'

An old woman shouted, 'But sir, what on earth will become of those poor souls who lived in the kingdom?'

'Oh, dear woman, you do not understand me. They are free. Free! Their own spirit will make them whole. Sirok will never be the same. For those who come to know Sirok, to *truly* know it, will be forever changed.'

The warrior looked down to his finger that bore a ring that sparkled in the morning light. He thought of the boy who gave up one treasure for another and he raised his chin with confidence. He gazed out to the souls who stood in silence and abruptly tugged on the reins. The stallion reared back on its hind legs and then, galloped at top speed up the rocky mountain."

TWO
Elias

His brush strokes touched the canvas like a breeze sifts through the morning mist. The bristles of his brush were worn and lost on previous paintings, but he felt in complete control as his brush was an extension of his fingers. With his right hand, he dabbed a speck of magenta and with his left, reddish-brown. With a wisp of a stroke, his imagination exploded as he could see a coiled snake on the other side of a fallen tree. Not far away from the rotting trunk, his mind created another tale of gypsies that plodded down the narrow trails below the hill. He was bringing meaning to a deep forest that was taking shape on the scuffed canvas. His images were fresh as he blended what he saw in front of him with what he could form in his mind's eye. It all lived in that moment but began a life of its own on the flat surface.

Elias tilted his head from side to side and inhaled the pure mountain air as he measured his progress.

Looking away at the rolling Mátra Mountain range, he could smell and taste a mix of deciduous beech and birch trees that sat on a draft coming from the east. *One day I'll catch this scent in a painting…yeah, I have to figure that out,* he thought.

When he had arrived a few hours earlier, the sky was a deep blue with only the faintest veil of clouds on the horizon that played with the smooth and rolling mountain crests. The heavens were now a smear of amber as the spectrum of colors gradually cloaked the sky. This moment was altogether different and new.

Perched high upon a cliff, he was alone as he swapped a blank canvas for what was becoming a kaleidoscope of the Hungarian landscape. This was his haven. He entwined himself with the beauty and love of nature. This was nothing new. From a young age, Elias knew what stirred his heart.

He made his own canvases by stretching remnants of an abandoned gypsy tent over a frame he made from a discarded crate. Nattymama, who was an herbalist, mixed and blended his paints using her own recipe. His brushes were horsehair affixed to slender but sturdy sprigs from a nearby cypress tree. Elias used forgotten wooden dowels and hinges he found and made them into a sturdy easel. This was all he needed.

Elias' long brown hair grazed his shoulders. His light brown eyes were striking and ominous to some but opened a gateway to a peace from deep within him. Lean and average height, he could be pensive and appear brooding at times. Although he was private and a little shy, Elias seldom kept his thoughts to himself if others pushed, teased, or tested him in any manner. Like his paintings, he was an original. He was an old soul who was true to his feelings. He was often frustrated that others didn't take their time to understand him.

Pausing for a while, he surveyed the vast and beautiful terrain, and he wondered what he could find if he went deep inside the forest well beyond the trees and rocks that were in plain view. He loved what he painted and allowed his imagination to fill in the blanks, but he wanted to know and experience more. The forest looked dark, dense, and cold, but that was just an assumption or a guess—he wanted to know for sure. He had never traveled the paths within. Papa cautioned him about the dangers, telling him he could enter at his own risk but it would be better, still, to leave the forest alone, as there was much to do right around home.

At ease with his own thoughts and feelings, Elias was happy and fulfilled, but he had a darker side too. An inner voice gnawed at him, reminding him that he was different from the others in his family and those in and around the village. He shared his feelings with only a few, but he always expressed himself in his work. As he pieced together in his mind who he thought he was and wanted to be, it was clear what caused the special beat in his heart and created personal joy deep within him.

*****

Elias' home and family farm were close to where he liked to paint. They lived about three kilometers from a small village. With three large rooms and a loft, Papa built their house of white stucco and a thatched roof. Various supporting buildings, including a small barn and a few sheds, completed their home.

Inside their home, the walls were pure white. Large exposed and rough beams separated the living area from the loft, where the children slept. The furnishings were colorful, like his palette, as were the meticulously crafted quilts and wall hangings Mama and other women in the family had embroidered. They delicately stitched them with intricate detail over many generations. One of Elias' paintings hung over the hearth at Mama's insistence. It was a warm yet functional home.

They grew wheat. Livestock on the farm included a cow, a few oxen, some sheep, chickens, and a rooster. Mama and Papa were raising three boys and two girls, and Elias was the second oldest boy at fifteen.

*****

Mama was headstrong and could be stubborn when she wanted. She stood on tiptoes to reach the pan, wiping her face with floury fingers. Wincing, she put her hand up, loosening the bun that seemed much too tight today. She had known Papa since they were both five years old. As was the custom, their well-intentioned parents had arranged their marriage long before they would even remotely notice each other.

Papa appeared older than his years. He had a full face and was balding, but what hair remained on his head was gray. A large man with big features, he always wore a hat to keep the rays of the sun off his head while he worked in the field. Although he surprised his family on occasion, he was a man of few words. The children noticed this as they yearned and competed for his attention—all but Elias. He treated his daughters like china dolls, but treated his sons like toy soldiers. He was gruff and said little to them unless it pertained to running the farm. This was not because he didn't want to, but because he just did not know how to.

Today started out like most others. Mama was the first to rise and spent her day cleaning their modest home, mending the family's well-worn clothes, and preparing all of the meals. Not so long ago, there were few modern conveniences in Hungary, especially on a farm.

Later in the day, Mama began preparing the evening meal. She carefully browned the beef chunks and began to place the first batch of meat in the bottom of her Dutch oven. She knew not to rush any part of the preparation of her family's goulash recipe. She knew it took time to simmer. She knew that beef only became goulash by taking the proper steps and adding the right ingredients.

"Where is Papa? He was supposed to be back by

now," Mama asked her two daughters as they helped her set the table. At that moment, Papa flung open the back door and entered with a box of supplies.

"Ah, my home is full of delight! That aroma, my little girls and you, Mama. Girls, give me a kiss."

Mama was not so easily won over. Tight-lipped, she put one hand on her hip, "There you are. Did you remember the paprika?"

"Yes, my sweet bride."

"Give me, give me. How about the sweet red wine? You know it cannot be *my* goulash without the sweet red wine."

"Yes, yes, I have the wine."

"You didn't loosen the lid and…"

"NO! Mama, I didn't. I don't like red wine anyway," he finished his sentence under his breath.

Mama eyed him suspiciously. "What did you say?"

"Nothing, nothing."

"Good. Now, sit down or do something. Keep yourself busy. The girls and I have things to do. You know this will have to simmer for some time?"

Papa sat in his chair, picked up a book off a small table next to him and began to read. After only a few minutes, his arms slowly lowered the book to his lap while his eyes closed. Mama continued working in the kitchen. Noticing the girls had completed their chores, she motioned them to her side.

"Girls, go outside and enjoy the last of the sunshine. It is my favorite time of day—it's when magic happens. Watch for your brothers." She smiled as they did as they were told.

Much to Mama's surprise, she heard Papa ask, "Where is that boy, Mama?"

"Kristof, Elias, or Jozef? Who are you talking about, Papa?"

"You know who I am talking about Mama— Elias! Where is he?"

"Whew! Did you have a bad dream or something? Finish your nap and don't get all stirred up," she said.

"No Mama, I've been meaning to talk to that boy."

"He's not a boy anymore Papa, please! He's growing up," she said.

"So he is. I'm sure he's loafing off somewhere," Papa was exasperated.

"He is out doing what he loves to do. I don't

blame him. He was up early and already finished his work for the day. Leave him be."

Papa slammed the book on the table, causing a stir, and stood up. He walked to the window and saw his two girls outside playing and laughing.

"Don't remind me! There is *always* work on a farm. The others are still in the field, I am sure of that. I have told him time and again to give up his selfish ways and pull his weight where he's needed."

Mama kept her back to him as she wiped the stove around the pot of goulash. There was a heavy silence. Finally, she turned and gave him a level look.

"Where HE'S needed, Papa? You have two other sons who wield a sickle just as firm and clean as Elias and they enjoy what they do. They may be in the field but you know that's because they love farming; you favor them." She slammed the drawer shut and banged the pans around. Turning, with a furrowed brow, she pointed a wooden spoon in his direction, "There, I said it! Leave Elias alone! You WILL push him away, I'm telling you. Is that what you want? I WON'T have it!"

Papa turned away from the window. He looked at Mama and waving his hands as if he was swatting a fly, he said, "NO! But enough about me pushing him away. You coddle the boy too much. You encourage him. He knows I don't approve of his pastime—it will never take him anywhere. It will only bring him heartache. You know that, Mama."

"HA! You don't *approve* of his pastime, you *deplore* it…and you say I 'coddle' him. How dare you! I do what a good parent should do—I reassure him and proud that I do."

Looking into Papa's eyes, she saw that she was not swaying him from his judgment.

"He needs to learn a trade if he doesn't want to be part of my farm. He should be a carpenter, or operate a machine, or …" Papa was relentless.

He walked over to where Mama stood, lifted the top off the pot of goulash, and sniffed the thick savory steam. He reached for a ladle as if their conversation was of the ordinary and dipped it into the rich gravy. Mama swatted his hand.

"Notions are already in his head, and your dear mother, Nattymama, listens to him too. Maybe *you* should listen to him as well." Mama cautiously worked her mother-in-law into the conversation.

"Oh Mama, you bring up Nattymama again. You always bring up Nattymama! I know he spends a lot of time down the hill in her cottage, but…"

Mama paused, walked to Papa and placed the palms of her hands on either side of his face. She looked squarely into his eyes and spoke in a harsh tone, "I bring her up, Papa, because she's good for the boy. She knows him. She believes in Elias."

Stunned, Papa sat down in his chair again and scratched his head, thinking about what Mama had told him. Thinking aloud Papa muttered, "You may just be right …" He brought his hands up to his face as if he were praying and again said, "You may be right …"

A moment later, Elias opened the front door as a gust of wind caught it and slammed it against the wall. As if Elias had lit a match to a fuse of dynamite, Papa went from thoughtfulness back to anger.

"So you finally decided to come home, did you? You must be hungry—or is it too dark to paint? What is it?" The disgust was evident in his expression.

"What are you talking about Papa? I always come home. Are you going to start with me again?" Despite his calm appearance, Elias felt the blood drain from his head and his stomach felt like a rock.

"How about we all wash up for supper? It will be ready soon," Mama interrupted, trying to regain peace.

"I'm not *finished* with Elias."

Elias felt ambushed and let out an outburst. "*YOU'RE* not finished with *ME*? What did I do?"

"You paint too much. You are now reaching manhood and you need to learn a trade *if* you want to go against me. That is, if you do not want to be a farmer…I can't support a dreamer."

"A dreamer?" Elias asked.

"Yes! I can't just dream up food for your stomach or dream up clothes for your back. Nor can you."

Taking a deep breath, Elias barely got his words out, "But Papa, I pull my weight around the farm. I'm not going against you. I don't understand!" Elias looked to Mama for support. She sat at the table and tried desperately to keep the tears back. It was all too much, and she wept into her hands.

"Yes, but you do not want to be a farmer. You want to be an artist." Turning to Mama, he asked, "Do we know any artists or sculptors or dancers Mama?"

She looked the other way and used her apron to

wipe her eyes. She stood and, without saying a word, walked to the stove to tend to the evening meal.

"Ah! I will answer for you, Mama—NO!" Papa turned to Elias and said, "You can't provide this family with anything! How will you provide for a wife and family of your own some day? It is a selfish life to lead. Selfish!"

"So you have my life all planned out? A wife…children? That's for me to decide not you!

Papa stood and walked in circles as he spoke. He found his way to Mama's chair by the hearth, looked at Elias' painting overhead and smirked. He reached for it only to hear Mama raise her voice.

"Don't even think of it. I am only warning you one time," she said.

Papa grabbed his pipe instead and as his hands trembled, he began lighting the bowl. As he puffed to ignite his pipe, he made a declaration.

"By the time you reach sixteen years old," he paused and puffed on his pipe before continuing, "you must decide how you will live your life so that one day you can support yourself and a wife and children."

"WHAT? That's in a month and a half! Forty

days, Papa!"

"Yes, I know. Plenty of time to decide! We will always have this farm. If you make the right decision, your brothers and I will build you a spacious bungalow down by the stream. You work the land, get married in a few years, you forget about this so-called 'dream', and you will be part of this farm. If not—I want you out, and I never want to see you again."

THREE

Brother's Keeper

That evening, the air was thick as winter mud. Unsure of the events that had unfolded earlier that evening, the children kept to themselves and didn't dare ask a single question it seemed. Papa made a point to speak to each child except Elias, and he did nothing to acknowledge his presence. Elias said nothing, ate very little and excused himself from the table before others were finished. He kissed Mama on the cheek and went to bed early. A house that was naturally full of smiles and laughter was more like a cemetery. All was cold and dark; Elias was alone.

The next day could not come soon enough. Everyone scurried to begin their day. They rose extra early to start their chores to wash away the bitter taste of the previous evening.

Mama told them it was best to get a move on at the first sign of the sun. She warned them that she checked all the signs and it was going to be a hot day.

She went on to tell them to expect sizzling temperatures. She was fearful that the clouds would not show up to hide the glare of the sun—not even for a moment. One of Mama's talents was accurately forecasting the weather and getting them all to understand the value of water.

Elias was the first of the children to get up and leave the house through a back door. Trying to go undetected, Mama watched him from the window as he walked from their home. Turning to Papa, she gave him a tongue-lashing.

"You'd better know what you have done, old man. You have a lot to think about."

Unable to look her in the eyes, Papa slurped black coffee from his stained mug and said nothing.

Later, out in the field, the distinct sound of sickles slashing through winter wheat broke the quiet of the muggy morning. Elias' two brothers worked on a plot of land down a hill and not far from home. Already dripping in sweat, Kristof, Elias' older brother by two years, grabbed as many stalks as would fit in his large hand and at about knee high, wielded his sickle, cutting them about six or so inches below his grip. As he had done thousands of times before, he tossed the harvested wheat into a large two-wheeled cart he painstakingly pulled around the field to collect their yield. Taking a quick breather when the large cart was almost full, he wiped the sweat from his brow with his muscular forearm.

With every full cartload, he paused to bundle what he gathered. With care and precision, he pulled a few wheat stalks from his pile to use them like twine to bind clumps of wheat. Finding stubbles of grass for anchors, he took each shock and stood them on end. With his last bundle, he looked out to the field and felt good seeing their hard work standing tall and gleaming in the sunlight.

Their sandy-haired youngest brother, Jozef, worked somewhat slower but was steady, as he was just learning his craft at the age of twelve. He worked one hundred paces from his brother. This was a prime position because he could watch Kristof with a quick raise of his head to study his technique.

Although the wheat was golden and the heads of each plant drooped down, Kristof would take a moment here and there to pluck out some grains from a plant and bite down on them. Papa taught his boys that if the grain cracked in their teeth, it was ready for harvest. He was a stickler when it came to determining the ripeness of his wheat. Too soft and malleable meant the wheat would be prone to rot if they harvested and stored it too early. If this were ever to be the case, the boys knew that the family would do without meat, new clothes and other basics every family needs. This would not be for a week or a month, but a season. The mere thought of this made Papa's heart race.

A couple of hours into their work, Kristof took a swig of water and glanced up at the sky. He felt the intensity of the heat building up by the minute. He called Jozef to join him for water.

"Drink up. It's a scorcher. It's time we take a break anyway."

They sat on one side of the cart that provided little but treasured shade. Kristof couldn't help wonder where Elias could be. He looked in every direction, shook his head in disbelief and turned his attention back to his younger brother.

"You're doing a great job, Jozef. You have come a long way from our last harvest. We will soon spend our time threshing all this wheat, and you know how much fun that is," Kristof said sarcastically. They both laughed.

"Yeah, I want to be just like you and Papa," said Jozef.

Kristof looked him in the eyes and tousled his younger brother's long, shiny hair with his dirty, calloused hand.

"That's good to hear, but don't forget about Elias. He can be a good farmer when he wants to."

"Oh yeah! I want to be like him, too," Jozef said with an innocent smile. He stood, brushed off his pant leg, and peered from side to side as Kristof wiped the sweat from his forehead. "Hey, Kristof, here he is now!"

Elias, out of breath, ran up to where they were. "I am so sorry. After last night, I woke up this morning and had to walk. I had to clear my mind. I must have gone ten kilometers before I knew it. Time got the best of me." Elias said catching his breath at the end of every sentence. Bending at the waist, he placed his hands on his knees, gathering his energy.

"Dinner was horrible last night and it wasn't

because of Mama's cooking. I heard about the fight you and Papa had before we all got home. He really came down on you but he IS right, you know," Kristof said firmly.

"Huh? What do you mean?" Elias stood straight and bristled at his brother's comment.

Taking his time, Kristof stood up and stretched his arms to the sky, massaging them to loosen his aching muscles.

"You heard me. He's right, Elias. You don't want to grow, harvest and thresh wheat your entire life."

"Well—do *you*?" Elias asked.

Kristof reached down, picked up his sickle, took about ten paces and swung it. He paused and looked at Elias.

"Yes. Yes, I can honestly say that I do."

"Me, too," said Jozef.

"I like being out here in the solitude, knowing that I can grow my own food and take care of myself. I feel good about what I can accomplish," Kristof said as he lightly swung the sickle landing it with ease on his shoulder. He looked to the far reaches of the field and continued, "On a breeze, when I look out on the waves of wheat, I see my gold. Acre upon acre of gold sprouting from the earth." Kristof looked back at Elias and said, "Besides, I like the hard work, and I'm good at it."

"Are you sure you're not just doing what Papa tells you to do?" Elias asked.

Kristof stiffened at the question. He attempted to hold back his anger but couldn't. "JUST DOING WHAT PAPA TELLS ME TO DO? Papa's a farmer. He showed me how to farm and I happen to like it," he said. "When I listen to myself, that's what I hear. My heart tells me that farming is for me."

"Sorry, I didn't mean anything by it. I don't doubt it, Kristof. You're good at it, and I can tell you love it," said Elias.

"But, brother, *you* are not so good at it—and it's only because *you* hate it," Kristof snickered.

Elias picked up a sickle, walked a few paces and, with a whip, he sliced through the air and asked, "So now what? What do *you* think I should do?"

"Elias, don't ask me. Ask yourself. You must sort through your own thoughts…and put that thing down. You're going to take my head off with that thing!"

"It's not so easy," Elias said.

"To take my head off?" Kristoff blurted out with a laugh.

"You know what I mean," Elias sulked.

"I know it's not easy, but maybe look at it a different way. It's probably not so much about what you *think* you should do, as it is what you *feel* you must do. But whatever you end up doing, I know you will always be Elias and that will never change. That's what's most important. But whatever you decide, I'm right behind you."

"Me, too," said Jozef.

"Look, Elias, we have you covered. Papa's getting older, and we can manage this place without you. But for today, Papa's going to be here soon. All three of us had better get to work, or we won't have a future to think about."

FOUR

Omens

A few days passed, and it was the day of the month when many who lived close to the hamlet ventured to the village square. Here, the villagers and rural folks would purchase, sell, or trade staples. It was a time to socialize. Most times, there would be a juggler or clown competing for everyone's attention. Musicians with all kinds of stringed instruments filled the air with a variety of sounds. Elias, on most days like this, collected several of his paintings he hid in one of the lesser used barns, and take them to the village for display. He bundled them together with twine and hiked the three-kilometers through the woods to set up his gallery hoping to sell a few paintings. He didn't care about the money so much, but he wanted to come home with some change in his pocket with hopes that if he did, Papa would come to understand and appreciate him. He realized, too, that he needed the odd sale here and there for his own good.

He grabbed his satchel and stuffed it with a penknife, a few coins, his paintbrush, a pencil, and a sketchpad. With his back to the open barn door, he looked around one last time to make sure he had all he needed. He turned only to see the silhouette of Mama standing in the doorway with a flood of sunlight at her back.

"Elias, are you going into the village today?"

"Yes, Mama. I am going to sell some of my paintings in front of the apothecary shop."

"I thought so. I brought you some goodies to take along. It is a three kilometer trip through the woods, and your Mama worries about you."

He paused and looked at Mama and gave her a wide smile. She reached out to him and they gave each other a hug.

"Thanks Mama. I'll be fine. I do this every month."

"I know son, but you are my precious Elias. You are special. One day you will know what I mean, even if you don't feel so special today. I know Papa was tough on you, but don't give it much thought. You go and enjoy the day, and we'll keep all of this a secret."

"Thanks Mama, I love you."

"Love you too, my little Picasso."

*****

Thunder from storms the night before had rocked the house and lasted for hours. Today the bright sun shone on every wonder of the world. Everything was clean. A soft breeze stirred the scents of wildflowers from the side of the path to an undeniable aroma of the ancient forest.

Putting his worries out of mind as Mama had suggested, Elias traveled the dirt path that many have taken to the village. The chill of the morning air was moving away to welcome the warmth of the day. Elias made frequent stops to rest allowing him a moment to look around and take notice of the curiosities of nature just to the side of the path.

He saw a golden eagle overhead that seemed to be following him. He wondered what perspective it might have from so high above. As he walked, he heard the rustling of leaves in the deep green brush. He stood still and peered to where the sound seemed to be coming from. He heard it again and looked from side to side. As the swoosh and swish of the grass became fainter, whatever was slyly moving around him was gone. All became quiet, like the clock skipped a few seconds, but Elias decided it was of no consequence.

Elias came upon a stream that he knew well. He knelt down and cupped his hands to form a bowl. As he drank, water gushed down the side of his face. Wiping his chin with the back of his hand, he noticed large roots of an oak clutched and crisscrossed the bank. Elias marveled at the way that something that appeared to be so tangled could be such a vibrant source for nourishment and life. He thought how lucky he was that he could move about while other life was destined to live in one place. This maze of roots depended on the stream, as did the other living things in the area. He paused to consider how his life was part of a larger scheme. This was Elias. The magnificence of nature and the beauty of how everything meshed to become one were always on his mind. The world was his symphony.

A moment later, Elias heard a stone whizzing by only inches from his ear. The sound split the air in half. He crouched into a ball and rolled behind a large tree.

Someone was putting muscle behind these throws

and was sending stone after stone careening his way. They were hitting all around him and ricocheting in every direction. As soon as he buried his head in his knees all was strangely still. Taunting laughter came from the school bullies and their heckling crowded the air. Their jeering was all too recognizable. Standing about twenty paces away were Milan, Aron and Laszlo.

"So Elias, how about playing football with us today?" Milan sneered.

"Ah, ah…not today. I've got things I need to do—thanks anyway," Elias answered.

"What did I tell you? He spends his time *painting pretty pictures*," taunted Aron.

"Yeah, we don't need him. I told you, he's different from us," said Laszlo.

"I bet he wouldn't know how to play anyway," said Milan. "Let's get out of here. We're wasting our time with this loser."

With that, the boys were gone. Elias turned to sit against the tree. Clenching his teeth, he pulled his knees up close to his chest, took a deep breath and cleared his mind. *I could run circles around them if I wanted to,* Elias thought.

After the boys were out of sight, he gathered his belongings and set out again toward the village. He walked a half-kilometer when sheer panic overwhelmed him. He reached down and couldn't find his canvas satchel. He picked up the paintings but his satchel was missing.

There wasn't much in it—just a penknife, a few coins, his paintbrush, pencil and sketchpad. What worried him was the small painting he had intended to give Nattymama later that day was also in the bag.

He peered over his shoulder and took in a deep breath. He shook his head and thought that the bullies must have stolen his bag. Unsure at best, he turned around and retraced his steps until he stood where he had drunk by the stream under the large oak. There was a ruckus in the brush nearby and Elias tensed up and looked in every direction. A large black dog with the biggest head he had ever seen darted out from the green brush. Shocked, Elias focused in on his drooling jaws and that's when he saw it—his satchel. A thousand thoughts filled Elias' mind but only one stood out like an erupting volcano.

Should I leave him alone or go after what is rightfully

mine? What am I thinking? That bag is a part of me and no beast is going to tear it apart, Elias thought.

Elias found a fallen branch at his feet, picked it up and began to slash the air as he would when wielding a sickle on the farm. The dog held tight to the bag and growled showing more of his sharp teeth. Elias stepped closer and smashed the branch on a large boulder, startling the dog. He dropped the bag and fled. Elias felt beads of sweat pierce his forehead and thought how easy that had been after all.

Whew! Good thing I didn't have to hurt that mutt.

Continuing on the road, he thought about how he had cowered from confrontation with the boys but now felt good that he had finally stood his ground.

FIVE

The Mysterious Traveler

Elias always set up his paintings in front of the apothecary shop. The owner, Mr. Varga, was a good friend of Nattymama's. Elias put all five paintings he brought with him that day on a ledge near the shop window. He sat on a small stool the owner always placed at the bottom of the ten steps leading up to the front door. Today there was a small table with a cup of milk and a napkin with some cookies. Elias smiled and looked up to the window but didn't see Mr. Varga. He took a sip and popped a cookie his mouth.

He reached down to his satchel. He felt around for his pencil and sketchpad and pulled them out. His eyes caught an old woman dozing on a bench and decided she would be the subject of his drawing. He tilted back on two legs of the stool with his back against the building and began to sketch.

Like clockwork, there were always the same three old men who sat outside a tavern next to the apothecary shop. They spent the morning playing backgammon and gulping beer. The men were loud and overbearing at times, but Elias tried to ignore their foul mouths—he knew his own mouth got him into trouble from time to time.

Mr. Varga was looking on. He hurried down the steps to where Elias was sitting and placed his hand on his shoulder, "Elias don't pay attention to those three bellyaching old, fuddy duddies. I've been listening to them for years. I liken them to a three headed, fire-breathing dragon we hear about in The Legend. You know what I mean—the dragon can only exist when it is spewing fire while the other two heads flail around. I'm telling you, they're obnoxious but harmless."

Elias nodded with a forced grin at the kind man and continued sketching the old woman on the bench. A few minutes passed and Elias noticed across the cobblestones a hunched over man was selling trinkets, jewelry, and odd little statues. Next to him was a woman who peddled blankets and other items she made. Further down the road were butchers and farmers who sold meats, eggs, and vegetables. Delicious wafts coming from the "soup lady" a few doors down made their presence known too. The aroma alone made his stomach growl. The ruckus of the vendors kept a buzz in the air, as did the murmur of the crowd. Normally, this narrow road saw few pedestrians, but on days like this, Elias thought this must be what it is like in Budapest or another large city. Elias could only imagine what life was like beyond the ten-kilometer circumference of his home.

After an hour or so later, Elias spotted a finely dressed, well-to-do lady weaving throughout the street browsing what others were selling. She wore a large hat with what appeared to be peacock feathers flouncing up and down as she strolled. Her dress was colorful but obviously worn. What struck Elias the most was her layers of costume jewelry and heavy makeup. She pulled her bright red hair up under her feathery headdress while stray hairs were stuck to her face.

She looks like someone who knows art, he thought, *I hope she comes over here.* As if reading his mind, the woman zigzagged her way over the uneven cobblestones and began scrutinizing his paintings. She broke her silence to comment on what she saw.

"Pretty things, but I don't know…I just don't

know." She looked up after a few minutes, and her eyes met his with an odd smile. "I presume you painted these?"

"Why yes, yes I did," he said, unable to hold back a proud smile from spreading across his face.

"Your use of color is interesting, but…I just don't know."

"What do you mean, 'You *just* don't know?'" asked Elias.

Bending slightly, she looked intently at a landscape. Keeping her back to him, she glanced back at Elias and arched an eyebrow. She said with a smirk, "Heavens, boy, are you talking back to me?

"Ah … ah, no. Of course not."

"Good because I could buy the whole lot of them if I wanted to. I want you to know that," she scoffed.

"Oh, I see. I understand. Are you some kind of art expert?" he asked with boldness.

"Watch what you say, boy! Your implication is as inappropriate as are your questions."

He turned and rolled his eyes and under his breath he said, "Boy, was I wrong about you."

"If you're looking to make a little money, I could

use some help around my house. That, dear boy, I would be willing to pay for," she said.

Elias folded his arms across his chest and shook his head. With an exaggerated sigh, the woman walked away with her nose pointing to the sky. Elias felt his heart pound but forced the event out of his head. He sat down and reached for his sketchpad.

Before Elias could put the point of his pencil on paper, a tall, thin, older man appeared from nowhere and began studying Elias' work. Elias kept an eye on him while the man spent, what seemed to be, a long time on each painting. Captivated by the man, Elias braced himself with what could come next.

The man, who had perfect posture, wore a small hat and had a long white mustache and a thinning beard. He observed each painting through small, half-framed glasses. Each wrinkle in his face was a roadmap to where his life's journey had taken him. As he approached each canvas, he moved his head back and forth and his silent and pensive gaze told a story. Elias just wasn't sure what the story was telling him. Each raise of his chin and tightening of his lips was clearly a new thought and a new paragraph. A squint of his eyes was another, as if he were actually spying directly through the painting and seeing something no one else saw. After examining the fifth painting, he pivoted toward Elias.

"You have brought me joy. These paintings are like no others I have ever seen. I feel the warmth of your sun. I smell the early morning dew and I am standing, yes, *standing* on that hill looking down on what is good," he said pointing to the bottom left painting. He turned back and held his palm open to Elias saying, "My boy, you paint with a golden brush."

Not knowing what to make of the man's comment, Elias shrugged and smiled. He was overwhelmed. The man's words were like none other he had ever heard to describe his work.

The stranger continued, "I see so much more than colors and images in these paintings. I see the soul of the painter, and it has touched mine. If only I could offer you money, but I have none. I can only offer you encouragement and the advice to follow wherever your heart takes you. I also send all good thoughts your way."

With those words, he turned and walked away.

"Wait!"

The man turned back. Elias reached for one of his paintings and placed it in the stranger's hands.

"Please, take this with you," Elias said.

"You honor me."

"No, *you* sir, *honor* me," Elias said.

"You know, my boy, our essence comes from the place we were all created. This is the crux of who we are and we should give the fruits of our talents to others. There is no greater gift. You have given freely to me. Thank you."

Elias nodded and smiled with great humility.

"There's something else!" Elias turned away from the man and bent down to his satchel. He pulled out the small painting he had planned to give Nattymama. As he rose and spoke, he pivoted in one motion to face where the man had stood. He said, "I have another painting I'd like to show…" His voice trailed off as he realized that the man was gone—he seemed to have vanished leaving no trace or hint.

Elias looked from side to side in shock and, a cold uneasiness covered him like a blanket of snow. He shook his head in disbelief. Shuffling his feet as he walked, he plopped down on his stool. Still puzzled, he looked around again. Scratching his head, he looked at his four remaining paintings and smiled. He thought how gratifying it felt to have talked to that man and how that special moment would last forever. Shrugging it off the best he could, he reached for his sketchpad and pencil. He plucked them from the ground and continued his drawing.

Mr. Varga stepped into the doorway and looked down at Elias. With all the commotion he heard to one side, he looked over to the tavern where the old men were playing their games, laughing and burping. He grabbed a broom that was leaning on the side of the door and began to sweep the landing to his shop. The three men guzzling beer and playing backgammon were getting louder and let their spirits get the best of them as they raised their voices so that Elias could hear their banter.

"Doesn't that boy know he's wasting his time?"

"If he were my son, I would set him straight. He's taking so much from his family—I know that family," one of the men retorted.

The third man, who had a long neck, folded his

arms across his chest. He frowned in disgust and shook his head. He turned and glared at Elias.

The first man added, "He should listen to that lady who came by earlier. I tell you, that boy's as crazy as his old grandma." Looking to continue his game and move his chip, he placed his index finger on one of his pieces, pulled it back and said to his friend, "Anyway, it's your move."

Elias felt his blood rush up to his face and his hands began to sweat. He kept telling himself to keep calm and to say nothing. The moment was getting the best of him and Elias couldn't take it any longer. Just before he was about to speak, Mr. Varga said, "No, sir, it's YOUR move." With disgust etched on his face, he glared at the man who had begun the attack. "You are nothing but a coward and a bully. You sir, should apologize to the boy."

"Never. It is not my way."

"You are to be pitied," said Mr. Varga. "I should've suspected that you were that kind of person."

"I'll apologize when he gives me reason to, but I'm sure that will never happen," the man said with a forced cackle.

Elias, with his eyes fixed to the cobblestone, packed up his belongings. Mr. Varga, who wanted to help Elias with his things, thought better of it and stood aside. As Elias began to walk away, he nodded to Mr. Varga and gave him a faint smile. It was then that he heard the revolting laughter and jeers start up again. He lifted his eyes to the blue sky and never looked back.

SIX

Nattymama

Most were wrong. Although old, frail and slightly hunched over, the villagers thought she was out of touch—even crazy.

Nattymama was a caretaker of life. Life fascinated her and her curiosity took her many places. She had forgotten more knowledge than what most people acquired during their entire life. She succeeded to keep her youthful spirit as she handled all situations as if they were new. Never did she use old ways to solve new problems. She would harken back, however, to "wisdom" to help navigate in the most wicked of all currents.

Imposing mountains bound her home to the east, and the dense forest surrounded her on the west. Meandering through her land was a stream. It was important to her as it reminded her of the life it sustains and the future it will ensure. Her modest dwelling and garden were set off the dirt road about one hundred and thirty-two paces. Those few who paid her a visit, she welcomed warmly.

One of the many doors in her home opened to a magnificent garden that was twice the size of her house. It was in the shape of a large circle with four smaller circles within the perimeter at equal distances. It had stone walkways twisting and turning on to each other and intersecting at the center. At its very heart was a huge compass and sundial. To Nattymama a compass was always important but couldn't care less about the time of day. What mattered to her was the sun itself and the sundial was her way of never forgetting that all relies on the glowing ball in the sky.

Her garden was a rendering of her soul. Some plots of herbs, where the ginkgo biloba and the Klamath weed thrived, were heavy with growth. In other patches where thyme and fennel grew, the plants were sparse. All together, the garden was glorious. She planted and nurtured countless varieties of herbs. Hemp seed, gynostemma, and fairy wings balanced the paprika, bay leaves, and blue poppy seeds. She called her garden Hope.

She took herbs and used ancient recipes, as well

as some of her own, to create elixirs. She blended just the right ingredients to ward off every disease, disorder, complaint, or weakness of the mind, soul, and body. She prepared special potions and uplifting mixtures as well. She was the last of a long line of herbalists who became, in a way, one and the same with their own mixtures. The same with her own ingredients, all of which she nurtured and grew with a delicate and caring manner. Her soft, arthritic hands managed to pulverize, mix, pinch, and caress each herb and plant so she could extract its very life to become something more when she mixed and blended it with others. Masterfully but cautiously, she knew how to locate the essence of what she grew and then carefully transform it, reaching a higher purpose, thus obtaining its ultimate potential.

Nattymama's home was sunlit and bright with many windows and doors in every direction. Her hexagon shaped bungalow teemed with books and artifacts from another time and place. Dried herbs hung from the dark beams above, and glass jars, ceramic containers, and an assortment of utensils, tools, and other odds and ends adorned the shelves and counters that filled her space. The most striking feature, constructed in the exact center of her home, was a large, circular stone chimney with several fiery openings. Oftentimes, the staccato glow from the blaze within danced wildly against the walls.

Most days, after Nattymama tended to her garden, she would sit on a stone bench near the stream. This was her spot to rest. She would spend time here to reflect on matters both important and trivial. She enjoyed hearing the water bubbling and gushing over the smooth, flat stones that did little to impede its flow.

"Nattymama! Nattymama!"

She heard her name called in the distance, but paid it no attention.

"Nattymama, where are you?"

She remained silent because she knew that Elias would find her; he knew where she would be at this time of day.

Elias jogged up and sat beside her. As if in meditation, she kept her gaze focused on the flow of the stream. Elias looked to the water and set his attention there as well.

Impatient, Elias spoke. "What am I supposed to do, Nattymama?"

With her unwavering eyes still focused on the flow of the water, she broke her silence. "Keep looking at the water as it flows. The water knows what it needs to do."

Puzzled by her response, Elias started again. "No, Nattymama. I don't know what I am to do with my life!"

"My answer is the same, Elias. Look at nature, and you will know how to lead your life."

Knowing that this was not the answer that would help him today, Nattymama thought it was time to try something different. She looked toward him and with her aged hand, she reached out and touched his chin. She forced him to look her in the eyes. Nattymama winked and tenderly spoke as her emerald eyes gazed intently into his.

"You tell me all that rests in your mind, what sits in your soul and all that dwells in your heart. Maybe your Nattymama can help."

"I feel so guilty," he sighed.

"Guilty! You have nothing for which to feel guilty. What are you talking about?"

"Papa tells me that I must be a farmer or I'm out

on my own—for good. He says I'm selfish and will amount to nothing as an artist."

"Oh, what does he know?"

"He told me that I must decide to be a farmer, learn a trade or consider myself shunned by him—all by my next birthday."

There was a pause. All they heard were the sounds of the gushing stream and a warm breeze flipping the leaves high above in the nearby trees.

In a quiet and somber tone, Elias spoke.

"You know, he might be right."

"Whatever are you talking about?" Nattymama said.

"Well, this lady came by and looked over my paintings. I thought she was interested in them. I thought she actually liked them. But she hated them. And then the old men drinking beer, they…"

"You never mind about those ugly men! I know those ugly men. Ugly!" she finished with a quick shake of her head.

"They might be right when they say I'm selfish and wasting my time. Apparently I won't amount to anything," Elias said.

She looked at him with soft smile and said, "Elias. Please do not pay attention to those ugly men. They sit around all day and say so little by saying so much. They are good for nothing. As far as your papa…well, he thinks he knows best, but he doesn't know any better. He only knows one type of man and one kind of life. That man doesn't know it but he has so much love. He will wake up one day. That I know, but enough about him."

Elias turned to her and asked, "Suppose I try to live my life as an artist and fail? They will all be right. *Papa* will be right. Maybe I *should* be a farmer, find a wife, have children, and try to be content."

"What? Elias, tell me something. What if you become an artist and *succeed*? You should ready yourself to answer that question, too."

Nattymama turned and looked away from Elias. The gush and gurgle of the water was, again, noticeable. She lifted her trembling hand and with three fingers pointed to the stream, poking the air, and peeked over at Elias.

"What was I saying? Oh yes, that stream is talking to us. Listen—can you hear what she is saying?"

He paused and smiled. "Nattymama, there was this one old man who liked my work. Someone I have never seen before in the village. He must have been a traveler."

She turned to him and said, "See, my boy? Listen and you will hear the stream."

"I gave him a painting."

"That is wonderful, Elias. Tell me about this man. What did he do? What did he say?"

"Well, he was very quiet and studied each painting up and down. He contorted his face and puckered his lips as he looked at one and then another."

"Did he look like this?" Nattymama twisted her lips and cheeks. Her eyes bulged out and her face turned red. They laughed. Elias' eyes sparkled as he nodded.

"Go on, Elias, tell me more about this gentleman," Nattymama said.

"I saw in his eyes something I have never seen before. I don't know exactly what it was, and it sounds bizarre, but I liked him."

"Go on, my boy, what else? What did he say?"

"When he finished looking at all of my paintings,

he told me that I brought him joy. I have never heard anyone ever say that. Well, except for you, Nattymama—and Mama. But, anyway, he told me that he had no money and wished me well. As he was walking away, I called him back and offered him one of my paintings. It was the best one I brought with me. He looked at me and told me that I honored him. *Think of that.* Before I could say anything else, he disappeared—just vanished. Poof!" Elias snapped his fingers.

"Poof?" Nattymama asked.

"Yeah, poof! You know, he was standing there one minute and gone the next," Elias explained.

Nattymama playfully slapped Elias on the shoulder and said, "I know what poof means." She smiled and continued, "Elias, tell me, what did this man look like?"

"Well he was tall, and…old."

"More, boy, more."

Elias pursed his lips and tapped the side of his head with two fingers and said, "Oh yeah, he had a long, gray beard and wore little eyeglasses on the tip of his long thin nose. It looked like he may have had long hair bunched up in some kind of strange little hat. It looked like a flower pot."

"Was this fellow tall and standing straight as the great oak on the other side of my garden, and did he have a raspy voice?" she asked, straightening herself as much as she could.

Yes! That's exactly what he was like Nattymama!" His face glowed as he answered.

"Did he seem forgetful?"

"I don't know about that, but we didn't talk too long. Do you know him?"

"Possibly. But that's neither here nor there. I know many souls from here and back again. Enough of all that…listening to you, I have an answer for you."

Elias asked, "You do? You know I trust you. I *knew* you'd have an answer for me."

"It is very simple…your heart will tell you. Follow your heart. Just as the water knows to flow, whether over stones or not, your heart will tell you how to live your life."

"Nattymama! I don't understand. I came to you for help and all I'm getting is some mystical mumbo jumbo," Elias said as he felt another blow to the gut.

"Elias, I don't know what you should do with

your life. Only you know whether you should be an artist, a farmer, or whatever. Your heart is your guide. That is all I can tell you."

Leaving Elias on the bench, Nattymama stood and walked into her house. She put a pot of water over the smoldering embers, and began chopping herbs on a nearby stone slab table. Elias followed her inside and sat in a large wicker chair. The air was teeming with thoughts but they both remained guarded. Nattymama was agitated and coldly tended to her task.

"What's wrong, Nattymama?"

"You ask, what is wrong? You place your whole life on my doorstep but want none of the risks and challenges I tell you about." She wagged her bony finger in his direction and continued, "How dare you, Elias! You do not like my answers," with short, abrupt moves, she quickly began chopping more green stalks of herbs. "You want everything to be easy. You want it given to you on a silver platter. I tell you, what is good comes with work. Work, I tell you! Sometimes a struggle as well," she said flailing her knife above her head.

"Oh, gosh, Nattymama, I'm so sorry. No, I'm just

confused. I want to make sure I do what is right. That's all."

"Right for whom? You want to listen to everyone but yourself. You tell me they 'might' be right about you. What do *you* say about you?"

The tension built as Elias sat in stubborn silence.

"You want to have a foolproof roadmap. No one has such a thing. That woman who you thought liked your paintings has no roadmap. The three ugly men definitely have no roadmap. Even Nattymama—no roadmap. Maybe you are not an artist and maybe you are. Maybe you are meant for something else."

"You're right. I need to find my own way. Maybe I haven't given myself a chance to know what my dream is." He stood and walked over to where Nattymama was working. "Maybe I can find my fortune and bring it home so Papa and Mama and the others will know who I am. That's it! Whatever it is, I've got to follow my heart to get to my dream. That's where my answer will be," Elias said.

Nattymama put down her knife and walked over to Elias. He didn't know what to think. She opened her arms to hug him and whispered in his ear, "Now you're talking." Nattymama kissed him on the cheek and as if nothing happened, she went back to the stone slab. She began to gather the small pieces she had minced, and said, looking down as she worked, "But do not confuse things."

"Huh? What do you mean?"

"It is simple. By following your heart, you will find your fortune. Your dream matters not, as many dreams are driven by something other than one's heart."

"Oh, I see," Elias said with no real conviction and dismissed her statement. Nattymama, knowing he did not hear her message, overlooked his youthful zeal.

"Well, let me continue. You have only been on a farm, in the mountains, and in one small village. My boy, you must go on a journey—a quest," she said walking two of her fingers in the air.

Elias was stunned. He was thinking figuratively, not literally. A thousand thoughts went through his head all at once. He returned to his chair, slumped in it, and was even more confused than before. Keeping calm, he respectfully asked questions.

"So, Nattymama, what kind of *quest* should I go

on? Where do I go?"

"You must go from here. Yes, you must go far from here."

"Why must I go far from here? Where do I need to go?"

"You are sure to find your answers by taking a journey. I can set you out on that journey, but I cannot tell you every footstep and turn to take. I can help you to avoid the pitfalls, but you will have to defeat the evils that keep you from listening to your heart and finding your dream. I cannot do those things for you, but you can. Are you ready to take that journey?"

Elias began to puff up like a balloon with each thought. He began to hang onto her words as she continued. He sat forward before standing up and then paused for a moment. He jumped to his feet and threw his hands high above his head and said, "Yes, Nattymama. I'm ready."

SEVEN

The Preparation

Elias left Nattymama's home re-energized. By the time he got home, his family had finished dinner and Mama and his two little sisters were washing the dishes. Papa was out in one of the small barns with Kristof and Jozef sharpening the sickles.

Elias apologized to Mama, and as he did, she wondered what was now different. She didn't press him, as she was just happy to see a gleam in his eye. Assuring her he was going to be fine, Elias excused himself, gave her a kiss on the cheek and went to bed early.

He slept about half of the night, but Elias made sure that he was the first one up before sunrise. He knew his family well, as it was much too early for anyone to be stirring—not even Mama. Quietly, he splashed cold water on his face, ran his fingers through his long hair, and got dressed. He tiptoed down the wooden staircase doing all he could to miss the spots he knew would creak. He grabbed a muffin left over from the day before and poured himself a cup of milk. Gulping it down and holding in a burp, he grabbed the knapsack he packed only a few hours earlier. He crept out of the house pulling the door and turning the knob a certain way so not to make a noise. He paused after only taking a few steps and looked back at the door he had just closed. He spun back around and at that second the horizon smacked him in the face as the sun was rising in a clear sky with streams of colors that fanned out like fireworks—only without the blasts. The coolness of dawn was already giving way to a warm day that would be full of his questions. The sounds of songbirds reminded him that he was not the only one awake and looking for promise of what the day would hold.

He walked around the house heading for Nattymama's cottage and there, sitting on a wooden bench, was Mama.

Startled, he said, "Oh...ah, good morning, Mama!"

"Good morning, my dear son."

"I'm going…"

"Shhh, say no more. I know where you're going."

With that, she handed him a canteen filled with water.

"Elias, take this for your nourishment. As your mama, I have nourished you since you were a baby and have done my best to keep your body, mind and soul together. As you sip, think of me. Stay strong and never let your canteen go dry."

"So you've spoken with Nattymama?"

"No, Elias, I am your mother. There are certain things I know. Now go. You must be on your way."

Elias bent over to kiss Mama on the cheek, turned away and began walking. A tear streaked down Mama's face as she watched Elias blend into the trees and tall grass.

*****

As he walked to Nattymama's home, he saw a monarch butterfly awkwardly fluttering in the unpredictable breeze. Oddly, the butterfly maintained its distance and seemed to be going on its own journey—a journey it naturally knew. As Elias approached Nattymama's cottage, so did his winged friend. When Elias stepped up to the front door, the butterfly veered away and continued on its way. Elias watched it until it was out of sight and then gently knocked on the old, scarred door.

"Come in, Elias, come in! I rose early to begin assembling a few things for you to take with you on your journey. First, let me look at you," she said, reaching for his hands. She held them, looked him up and down, and said, "I'm glad you finally made it. We have much to review. Sit down Elias and pay attention. I will go over what you need to know, and don't ask me a lot of questions."

Elias sat on a tall stool next to where Nattymama was working.

"Now, since you are going to take this journey, I have some things to tell you and they are very, very important."

"Okay, I'm ready. I've brought a few things myself, if that's okay?" asked Elias.

"Why, yes! What did you pack?"

Elias began to pull open his knapsack, and inside were his sketchpad, pencils, a change of clothes, dried meats, and the canteen.

"I see you have canteen—that is good." Reverently she nodded and winked.

Elias began to repack his gear when Nattymama

began talking.

"Now where should I begin?"

"Your journey must begin from where our family originated. You must begin your travels at the ruin of the Castle of Sirok."

"Sirok!"

"Oh yes. Sirok—our very own ancient and mystical castle on the edge of the village."

"I don't know about that. I don't like what you've told me about the place. You know, The Legend?"

"You don't know the half of it, Elias. Yes, it is at the pinnacle of a three-hundred-meter rocky plateau. Yes, our ancestors carved it out of the rock. Yes, the views of the Mátra Mountains are spectacular," she said, as if she were a tour guide. She sat down in a large chair by a window, folded her arms and sighed. Elias followed her and looked out the window to see the mountain where Sirok stood in the distance.

"But, Elias, as lore has it, Sirok *is* a congregation of souls of all humankind—those who believe one thing or those who believe another or even those who only believe in themselves. It's not exclusive in the least. It is where worlds meet I like to say."

He turned to her and shook his head. "EXACTLY! That's the part I know about. Nattymama, we were told never to go there. YOU told me never to go there."

"I've changed my mind. I am telling you that you *must* go there now. You must! No journey is worth taking unless you know where it is you began. This is where *you* began."

"But it's where spirits and ghosts live," Elias said in a monotone.

"Yes. If you believe in that sort of stuff…which I do."

"Well, we have always been warned never to disturb that place."

"Again, you are correct, Elias. But you must put away such thoughts, as you will find more than just one occasional spirit stirring in the night during your journey or your lifetime. Enough said about that."

"I'm not sure I understand all this, but…"

"Precisely. Say no more. If you understood today, you would not be taking this journey."

"Well, okay, but I'm not much of a mountain climber."

"You *will* be, and you'll be much more by the time your journey is complete. You must arrive at the ruins by dusk tonight—my favorite time of day—and will continue your travels at daybreak."

Puzzled, Elias shrugged and raised his hands. Shaking his head in disbelief, he sunk low in a fluffy chair by the hearth. He reached for a loose vine of an herb that was hanging from a hook above his head and began to wrap it around his finger. He heard about every other word she said at that point, as the visions of ghouls floating in his mind sucked up most of his attention. Nattymama continued to speak as she moved around the cottage. She was pulling together what seemed to be random artifacts from different parts of her home. Letting out a deep breath, Elias looked on.

"So tell me, why must I stay overnight?"

Stopping in her tracks, Nattymama turned to him, put her hands on her hips, and said, "I see you are still having problems with spirits. Dismiss those thoughts now," she said firmly.

Elias shook his head and folded his arms. "Okay, okay. I'll ask no more."

"Good. Now just remember, it is your birthright.

My boy, you must always remember what is yours, or someone—or some*thing*—*will* snatch it from you," she said as she waved her open hand above his head and concluded by grabbing a tuft of his hair.

"Ouch! I said okay."

"You must be there by twilight as this is the only time you will be able to uncover the direction you must take in the morning."

"Uncover the direction I must take? I thought you were going to tell me that."

"This is extremely important. Please listen. As I said, when you arrive at dusk, you will find the three arches. Line them up in your view, and as twilight unfolds, you will see the moon hanging low in the sky through the third arch. Below the moon, you will see a path in the distance. It will be clear as day. DO NOT TAKE THIS PATH. You must forge your own way, but you may start where that path enters the woods to continue your journey."

"Ah, ah—okay."

"Then—are you listening?"

"Yes, Nattymama."

"You will see the moon pass through the third

arch as it climbs into the sky. It is at that moment you must go to the base of the third arch. Looking east, kneel down and run your fingers over the mortar that connects the stones. Pull the loose stone from the base and you will find something there that will help you with the rest of your journey outside of Sirok. It is of no use in the ruins. Remember the order of these events. That is crucial. You must safely return what you found before you venture home."

"Nattymama, what is it? What will I find?"

"It is always good to ask questions—except for this time. You are asking too many questions of me. I can only tell you so much as you must find the answers for yourself. *Trust me.* You will know-it-when-you-see-it," she said emphasizing each word.

"Okay, I-got-it."

Without giving Elias as much as a displeased look, she went on, "Good, good…VERY good. Knew you would." She went on to tell him that he must travel to Budapest to meet Zoltan, who was a cave dweller outside of the city.

"He has knowledge for all those who ask him about their fate. Zoltan is a Taltos."

Elias looked confused, so Nattymama continued in a rapid monotone. "You know? He is a Taltos, which is a messenger of the Creator of the Cosmos who can see in our hearts and guide us to what is rightfully ours. I thought everyone knew that," she said with a quirky smile and shaking her head. "He's a sorcerer."

"Ohhh," he said, with a hint of skepticism that Nattymama would not acknowledge.

"You will know him when you see him. Trust me. He will show you the way to the fortunes that you will find in Budapest. Trust Nattymama."

Elias wanted to believe. He knew that Nattymama would not steer him wrong.

"You will encounter many obstacles during your journey. It is inevitable because all journeys are eventful or they are for naught."

"Huh?"

"…or the journey is no good. As I was saying, I do not know for sure what those challenges will be, but you will be faced with situations that you must overcome, or you will be overcome *by* them."

"What kind of obstacles?"

"From here to Zoltan the terrain is treacherous,"

Nattymama said as she walked back to the stone slab where she was working.

"Can't I take the path that is clearly marked?"

"You can take that path, but that is the path most men take. Most men never know what is true but depend on others to carve the way. They take the easy path or route because they presume this will bring them the gratification and glory they seek. They never follow their own dream but follow someone else's misguided one," Nattymama said in a serious but mystic tone. "So take it, if you wish."

"No, no. NO. You've convinced me. You have always been right."

"No, my son, that is not true. Nattymama has been wrong. Don't worry…this time I know." She looked at Elias with conviction. A heavy silence hung in the room.

"So, Nattymama, getting back to the dangers—tell me about them," Elias said to break the quiet.

"You may encounter a Vadleany. You know a Vadleany is coming because you hear a distinct rustling of the forest leaves. She attempts to steal your…your… just beware," she said thinking better of giving him extra information.

Elias felt his face tighten and ran the palm of his hand over his head. He shook his head in disbelief but said, "I believe, I believe." He couldn't hide his youthful skepticism. His patience failed him and he blurted out, "Please, Nattymama. There's no such thing as a Taltos or a Vadleany or anything else. If I need to talk to this man named, Zoltan, then it makes no sense to create a fairy tale. I'm not a kid anymore."

Nattymama stopped what she was doing, turned, and looked directly in his eyes. Time froze. Almost inaudibly and in a whisper, she said, "You may leave now. Please leave. Go home and become a farmer. I am not holding you back. I told you that I cannot give you answers, but I can tell you how to find them. One day you will realize this is better. You have the choice. Believe and listen, or *leave* at once."

Like a dull knife, that moment pieced right through him. He hated himself more than any other time in his life. Shameful of the disrespect he had shown Nattymama. Elias lowered his head.

"Please forgive me. I'm so sorry Nattymama. I'll listen…and do what you tell me."

"Good," she said harshly. "No more petulance. I don't like petulance. Just don't like it."

She peered at him and frowned. He had never seen her wear that expression before. She was silent and walked slowly to a chair and sat. Her gray and white tabby jumped into her lap, nestled his head into the crook of her arm, and began to purr.

"Do you see this old cat? He knows who he is. He knows his essence but, then again, he has no choice. He has no choice whatsoever. He does not have a brain full of clutter. I would say that he is a happy little creature, and he keeps me company. Wouldn't you?"

"Yes, he's very happy, but what does this have to do with me? I said I was sorry," said Elias.

"Yes, I know and I accept your apology but please hear me out. Simple as my precious fur ball is, he has something that you cannot find in yourself. Oh, it is there, but so well hidden that only with your experiences will you truly understand what it is. Humans allow so much to cloud our essence that we live without our true selves. But just like my cat, we do not have a choice in the matter. We think we do, but our essence is who we are and our choices take us away from what the cosmos has given us. Do you understand?"

"I'm not sure. I've never been compared to a cat before."

"Oh goodness, my boy you have much ahead of you, however, you do make an old lady smile."

They both smiled as the cat jumped out of Nattymama's arms into Elias' lap. They chuckled.

"Listen to me now, Elias, so you can be on your way. The Vadleany is just one of many creatures you might encounter. But beware of the Sarkany I tell you—the *Sarkany*. Whew!"

"The Sarkany?"

"Oh yes, the Sarkany. It is a three-headed serpent dragon that becomes our worst nature. *Your* worst nature. It becomes what you loathe. It drags you down to the lowliest creature that exists in the Under World. *Ordak!* The evil one himself."

Elias felt alone as he listened to Nattymama. *The Evil One, as in the Legend?* He asked himself. Was the villagers'gossip true? *Was* she crazy? Although he didn't want to admit it to himself, this notion distracted him. He was confused, but his love for Nattymama was pure and he kept a mask of a smile on his face. He thought that he would set out on this adventure, and no matter what he did or didn't encounter, he would travel to Budapest out of love for her. He may not believe in these creatures, but he believed in her. He knew that she believed in him.

"Okay, Nattymama, tell me more," he said as he reached out and hugged her.

"That's the spirit, my young Elias! There are some things you may count on during your journey; one is the flight of the Turul. Follow her. She will never lead you astray. She will guide you to the Tree of Life. Once there, you will easily find Zoltan."

"Tree of Life?"

Nattymama gave a crooked smile, raised her arthritic fingers to her chin, and began to walk around her cottage. In all, she circled it three times. "*This* question of yours, my dear Elias, I will answer."

Elias felt he had better listen.

"See, my boy, the world is divided into thirds: the first being the Upper World where the Creator of the Cosmos and all her, or his, minions live. The Middle World is for us mortals, and the Under World is where the Evil One, Ordak, rules. In the very center of this stands the Tree of Life and it is part of all worlds."

Apparently exhausted, she sat in the chair by the window and waved her hand, capturing a breeze that flowed through her window. Elias stood, pulled a stool over to where she was, and sat in front of her.

"So, Nattymama, we live in the Middle World, but my journey will take me to the Under World?"

"Perhaps. I just can't be sure as it all kind of blends together sometimes. Don't worry about it. We all get a glimpse of the Upper World when we are open to it. It happens only for brief moments, so catch it and keep it close," Nattymama explained.

Elias was now more confused than before but he was fine with the feeling and what she told him. Nattymama walked over to a large chest of drawers and began rummaging through one drawer and then another. She walked across the room and began looking through decorative wooden boxes. What was once a tidy dwelling was now a mess.

"What are you looking for?"

"Ah yes, here it is."

"What is it?"

"This is an amulet that you must wear around your neck. Never take it off. You must have it when you meet Zoltan. He knows this symbol. It will protect you. This gold amulet is made of a special alloy, and its symbol is vital in your quest."

She handed him the amulet. It was four circles within a larger circle held together by twisting and intersecting horizontal and vertical lines. Elias examined it. He walked to the window and held it up to the sunshine. It was radiant. He again looked to Sirok and sighed.

"Wear it around your neck so it's close to your heart. It will not only protect you but will also remind you that your journey is to understand your true self and this is what you need to guide you to your treasure."

*****

Elias placed the amulet over his head and tucked in his chin to see it against his chest. He patted it a few times as if to make certain it was there to stay. With only a few other rations that Nattymama had given him and much to remember, Elias kissed Nattymama on the cheek and walked to the door. He turned to her and opened his mouth, ready to speak, but Nattymama shook her head and smiled. With her palm facing the floor, and in silence, she motioned to him to be on his way by wiggling her fingers.

"I will talk with Mama and Papa. Now go."

As he turned and faced the door, she smiled and blew him a kiss.

With his back to her, he said, "Thank you."

Elias walked outside and closed the creaky door. He gazed to the east and surveyed the mountain that was home to Sirok. It was not a high mountain, but it was steep with jutting crags and crooked cliffs that made him wince. The day had turned cooler and the warmth of the sun hid beneath a gray and threatening cloud that blanketed most of the sky. With only his small knapsack, he began his journey toward Sirok. He noticed another butterfly—perhaps it was the same one he saw earlier in the day. Pausing once more, he thought of what Nattymama said about the Upper World. He, then, looked to the mighty castle ruins that appeared only slightly larger than his own fist. He trekked on.

Instead of taking pleasure in the beauty around

him, as was his way, Elias turned inward. Bewildered with what had happened over the last several days, he wondered if this journey was going to help him. Would his quest truly provide a glimpse of what would make a difference in his life? As he walked, he placed his hand over the amulet that hung close to his heart and took it in his hand. He held it away from his chest and examined it yet again. Thinking about its significance, Elias thought about its unique design, which was nothing like anything he had ever seen.

EIGHT

Sirok

Before long, Elias found himself at the foot of the mountain. Looking to the peak and taking a deep breath, he began to hike up a winding path toward its summit. Halfway up, he felt the sting in his thighs and calves from the steep ascent. From his current vantage point, he could no longer see the ruins. Without seeing his destination, he somehow knew he was on the right course. As he came to a fork in the path, he didn't know which way to turn for certain, but he took one path over another only on a whim. As he continued upward, the terrain became rockier and unfamiliar. His footing, at times, was less than sure. He felt flushed, and sweat poured from under his brown hair and rolled down his cheeks. His heart raced with each step he managed to take up the steep and gritty path. He grew tired but pressed on as he felt the sharp rocks through the soles of his worn boots.

A stab of self-doubt overcame him but he dared

not to look down and kept his gaze upward. He felt alone and thought about backtracking. With every step, the amulet swung up and down, pounding onto his sweaty chest. *Thump, thump, thump.* His heart throbbed, and with each thump of the amulet, it reminded him of Nattymama's message. His doubt dissolved and he pushed on.

He stopped and rested along the way wetting his mouth with drops from his canteen and as he did, it sparked the thought of Mama's sweet smile. As he trudged on, even the smallest of pebbles under his sole caused him to lose his footing on the path. He searched for brush and jutting rocks to grab onto helping him with his climb as he neared the apex of the mountain.

Finally reaching the summit, he got his first close-up look of Sirok. Although it was in ruins, it was magnificent. He couldn't help but imagine what the walls once looked like. It stood faded against the sky with only a faintness of decoration still present on some of the walls. He thought of what life might have been like nearly a millennium ago when this fortress was crawling with people. What were they like? Who were they? What kind of dreams did they have? After his initial surge of enthusiasm, he dropped to his knees and sat back, exhausted. He rested.

After hundreds of years, Sirok continued to command a physical presence as its lore lived on. Huge, grey boulders outlined much of the area and marked the boundaries between safety and threat. Some buildings made of stone were intact, and a few graves were nearby. Wild and wiry brush now grew from the chinks and fractures in its courtyards and walls. This new kind life replaced the old, as it was all that appeared to remain of this ancient society.

The clouds lifted as the late afternoon sun began to shine through. Hints of deep reds and purples framed the heavens. Elias, now fully rested, knew he had work to do before evening fell. He decided to take a closer look at his surroundings. He figured he should find the first of the three arches that Nattymama had told him about. Twilight was coming fast. Behind a wall, he discovered what he thought must be the first of three arches. It was gigantic. Elias raced toward it. He could see the second and third arch in clear sight. Like a surveyor, he lined them up, and although it was not yet night, he saw the hint of the full moon hanging in the third arch. He scoured the horizon and saw a path—the path *not* to take—into the thick and dark woods. He memorized the position of the moon and landmarks to guide him.

The moments between light and dark were looming as he kneeled at the base of the third arch. His fingers gently traced the seams of the stones and the mortar that held the structure together. He detected nothing out of the ordinary. Going to the other side of the arch, he tried again to work his fingers into any crack or grooves he could see or feel. Making no progress, Elias paused to regain his bearings. He reached into his knapsack, pulled out his penknife, and began to outline the mortar around the stones. As he did, the cement turned to sand. He wedged his fingers into a crack to make the opening larger. He propped his feet up in front of him and against the wall for leverage. With all the strength he could gather, he pulled the stone toward him. Taking a quick breath, he looked inside and saw nothing. Knowing that the moonlight was now outweighing anything the sun could offer, he hunted through his knapsack and pulled out some wooden matches. Fumbling, he lit one and held it at the opening. This time, he saw a shiny, long item. The match burned down nearly singeing his index finger and thumb so he flicked it aside. In the emerging glow of the moon, he focused and tried to make out the object. He couldn't, as it was too dark. Extending his arm as far as he could reach, he was able to grab the object. Still unsure of what he was grasping, his fingertips told him that it was cold metal. Pulling it out to the open air, he was astounded at what he had uncovered. It was a sword.

Looking over the weapon, he realized that the symbol on the amulet was identical to the one on the sword's handle. He jumped up and stood straight with his feet firmly on the ground. With two hands, he raised the sword to the twilight sky.

"YEEEESSS!"

NINE

Quest

Night came only moments after his celebration. Elias made a small fire near a stone alcove that supported a slight overhang. He pulled the paper from the bread and cheese he had packed, slapped them together, and took a bite. He drank from his canteen. It was so quiet he thought he could hear the twinkling of the stars. Nearly choking on his sandwich, an owl startled him as it spoke to the dark sky with an unnerving hoot. The air was still. He thought of home.

Exhausted from his long trek that day, he lay flat on a bedroll and stared at the unspoiled sky and its many constellations. He felt as though he was so high and close to the heavens. Everything seemed clear to him. He reached upward to the illuminated heavens as if he was trying to touch the soft specks of light. A few falling stars grabbed his attention, but the moon sat as a large orb and appeared to rule the cosmos. He thought, *Where am I going? What's out there?* His eyes grew tired and he was soon asleep.

*****

"What the heck?"

Elias awoke to a dog's tongue lapping his cheek. Like a bolt of lightning, he sat up and used his sleeve to wipe off the unwanted saliva. Focusing on the guilty party, Elias realized the dog was the same one that tried to run off with his satchel days earlier. This time Elias was to discover that the dog dropped a pouch of food, a canteen of water and other items at his feet.

Elias grinned as he looked at the gifts and then at the dog. He shook his head in amazement. Rubbing the dog's head, Elias began to scratch him behind his ears. The dog laid down beside Elias and enjoyed being the center of attention.

"Maybe we're meant to be friends. What's your name? Hmmm, you've got to have a name. Let me think of a good one for you…I know, I'll call you Cimbora—my companion. That's it. Cimbora. Hey, boy, do you want to go on a journey with me? I'm pretty sure I'll need someone as resourceful as you on this trip. But don't get me in trouble with your habit of confiscating others' belongings," Elias laughed.

It was a bright and clear morning. Elias pulled his sketchpad and pencil from his pack, sat on the highest point of Sirok, and began to draw. With each shape he drew, he felt more excited about the unknown. Having difficulty concentrating, Elias hopped down from his perch, walked through the arches, and stood on the edge of the ruins. He could see for miles in all directions. At that moment, a warm breeze stirred. He saw the village beneath him and the many farms that dotted the landscape. He saw the beauty in the winding roads and the lush foliage from a new perspective. He knew where he stood was only the beginning of his journey, and answers would be unveiled in time. He was ready.

*****

After only a few hours into his journey, Sirok was now a memory. Elias traveled the path alongside the woods thinking he was leaving Sirok for good. The road he traveled was narrow and just barely wide enough for one farmer's wagon to pass at a time. The day was warming up, but Elias only sipped from one of his canteens occasionally, ensuring that he always left some behind. However, he worried about how he and

Cimbora would eat over the days ahead.

He's a survivor. He must know how to get food, Elias thought, especially since the dog looked healthy and well fed.

He knew he would have to leave the road and enter the woods at some point but figured something would show him the way. Using the mountains to one side and the sun to guide him, he knew what direction to go.

He began to think of Mama and Papa to whom he did not say good-bye. Nattymama promised him that she would wait a day to tell them that he had left but would return. With his thoughts moving from the faces of his family to the path he traveled, the joy he felt the night before was now waning hour by hour. Feeling its weight, he looked at the sword. *Will I really need this thing?*

Another few hours passed, and Elias was tired and hungry. He forged ahead although his pace slowed. He saw a small bridge over a stream in the distance that meandered through a small canopy of trees. With newfound excitement, he rushed to the base of the bridge, knelt down beside the stream, and splashed water on his face. He cupped his hands to drink. Cimbora joined him, and they had their fill. Elias pulled off his boots, rolled up his pant legs, and waded into the cool water. He thought that the stream might be the same one that meanders through and gives life to Nattymama's garden. He was refreshed.

Choosing exactly the right tree, Elias sank into the ground, leaning his back against a mighty trunk. Yanking open his knapsack to pull out his rations, he began to eat. He fed Cimbora knowing his supply was shrinking fast. He was not ready to pack up and continue his journey so he decided to take out his sketchbook and draw his surroundings. He sketched the stream bubbling over a log, the willow trees gracing the stream, and Cimbora relaxing in the shade.

Moments later, a man in a horse-drawn wagon pulled up beside him.

"Hello, young man. Are you lost? You don't appear to be from around here."

"No sir. I am on my way to find my…" Elias stopped short.

"Yes, go on," the man said as he took off his hat to wipe his brow.

"I'm on my way to find my, well, my fortune. I'm traveling to Budapest."

"Budapest! You've got a ways to go."

"I know, sir," Elias said as he looked away and to the horizon.

"So, it's your fortune you're looking for, huh?"

"Yes," he said with little hesitation.

"You sure about that?"

"Oh, yes. Yes, that's what I'm looking for," Elias said with more confidence, as he looked straight at the man.

With a wink, the man said, "Well, how about you and your dog climb up here and begin earning your fortune by helping me for the rest of the day. It will get you fifteen kilometers closer to the city, and if you work hard, I'll give you something to eat and a place to sleep for the night."

"Oh, I don't know."

"Well, by the looks of you, I'd say you're not going to make it there anytime soon unless you take advantage of the kindness of others."

Elias thought for a moment and smiled reluctantly. "I think you might be right."

"Climb on."

The rickety wagon seemed to move at a slow pace, but it was a welcome relief for Elias. The man introduced himself as Janos. He was a tall, lanky man with a closely cropped beard. Elias and Janos began to talk after an awkward period of silence.

"So Elias, why's a young man traveling with a sword these days?"

"It was a gift from my Nattymama who asked me to take it with me. It's one of those things that are passed down in families like a…like a…"

"Like an heirloom?" asked Janos.

"Yeah, that's it."

Janos turned his head to Elias and gave him a wink.

"If you don't mind telling me, what were you sketching on that pad?"

Surprised by the question, Elias was not sure how to answer. He knew, however, that he didn't want to hear another's judgment of him or his passion.

"Oh…nothing. I was writing a letter, that's all." Elias said, keeping his talents to himself.

"I see. I thought you were sketching these

beautiful hills. I've never seen anyone write a letter on paper that large. At least no one around here."

"It's all I have sir. I'm making due. So what do you do?" he asked to deflect the attention Janos was giving him.

"Ah…very happy you asked. I produce the best Hungarian wine in the country, I've heard tell. That's what you will help me with today—as long as you wish."

Janos owned a vineyard and operated a winery. He lived comfortably, near his vineyard. His home was off the road and into the woods. Without a family, he employed a number of men to work the fields and operate the winery. Knowing nothing about wine, Elias was intrigued.

"Was your father a winemaker?"

"Oh, no. He liked to drink it though."

"So why wine? I mean why did you choose to spend your life making wine?"

"Many years ago I left my home and was walking down this very road. Unlike you, I didn't know where the road was going to lead me. A kind man stopped me and offered me a job at his vineyard. And that, my young friend, was sixty years ago."

"Now you own it?"

"Yes, I now own it," Janos said with a kind chuckle.

"I hope I find my fortune like you."

"I did find my fortune, but it isn't what you think. My workers today, many of whom were like me when I was young, had no direction. They have joined me, and they work hard. Well, most of them. As they toil in the fields and in the winery, they help bring a plant from a vine to a fruit. As we do this in all our life's endeavors, we gain something within, and I have gained so much. With few questions, I give them a chance. Some take advantage, and others do not."

"What happens to those who leave?"

"Some come back to this road while others go deeper down the dirt path and into the woods. My home and winery are off that path. That's the way to Budapest."

Janos looked into Elias' eyes and smiled. Elias couldn't help but smile.

It was quiet with the exception of the clomping of the horse's hooves and the old and unpretentious wagon clanking and clattering on the rocky highway. Elias leaned back and closed his eyes. Some time had passed, and Janos barked out a welcome to some of his field workers. Startling Elias, he leaned forward. Janos pointed out his vineyard ahead of them. Its boundaries were difficult to distinguish. As they rode closer, Elias saw many more workers handling a number of different jobs. Some were harvesting grapes. Other workers were carrying lugs of grapes to wagons and still others were tending the vines with a delicate and precise touch. Janos pointed to one side of the vineyard to a road that veered off into the forest. He told Elias that a short way down that road was his home and winery. Just as soon as Janos finished his sentence, Elias saw a large bird circling the area.

"Janos, look! Is that a Turul?"

Janos looked up, but the bird disappeared behind a tree. His forehead wrinkled and he pulled on the reins to stop his horse. He looked at Elias.

"A Turul? We haven't seen a Turul around here in years. In fact, I think they're all gone. Boy, what do you know about the great Turul?"

"Nattymama told me about the Turul. They help

travelers find the right way."

"I wish I had a Nattymama. She sounds like a special person," he said.

"Oh, she is."

"Giddup Lucy!" Janos said as he gently waved the reins grazing the horse's side.

They continued off the main road onto the wooded dirt path. The trees that lined the road were tall with thick gnarled boughs. He had never seen trees like these before. The overgrown and oddly shaped leaves fluttered and stirred as the breeze whipped through the limbs, leaving a sweet scent behind. Together the branches, large and spindly, weaved a canopy above. As the sun's rays were now dappled, its light bounced as it created images all around as Elias and Janos continued on their way.

Moss-covered boulders dotted the landscape, and a winding stream bubbled and gushed over colorful stone surfaces. Noticeable eddies marked the bends of the stream capturing leaves, insects, and other small objects sucking them into each vortex. Elias' head spun to take in all he could while Janos stayed quiet with his eyes fixed on the path.

As if devised by some other power, Elias knew this entry into the forest and all he was experiencing conspired together to help him on his journey. He knew that he had made the right turn.

*****

Janos assigned Elias his duties as soon as they arrived. Once he gave some brief introductions, Janos left for home. Elias spent the rest of the afternoon working with a man named Viktor. He held the rank of winery helper, which was only a rung above cellar boy – Elias' job.

One large building at the winery housed the grape presses used to crush and press thousands of grapes. Most of the presses were enormous and needed several workers to operate. Some of the older presses needed only one person to run. None of this mattered, as Elias' job was to clean the floors around these machines.

The stained floor and soured grapes gave the air a rich tang. Elias was continually busy as other workers carried lugs of grapes and were not careful. Like an endless cycle, by the time Elias mopped the floor, more grapes dropped under foot only moments after Elias' last mopping.

Everyone had a duty to perform. It all started with those in the field who irrigated, pruned, and harvested the grapes when ripe. Following the process from picked grape to wine was fascinating to Elias. He appreciated the way that something as ordinary as a grape could serve the world from the commoner to the Pope in Rome.

*****

Viktor was several years older than Elias was, and he looked so much older. He was tall with dark curly hair. His eyes were so dark that his pupils were barely noticeable. He had missing teeth and a number of discolored scars that encircled his neck; no one dared ask about them. A wanderer, Viktor had only been at the winery for a few weeks, but the other workers already knew him for his gruff exterior and his sullen manner.

Viktor and Elias worked side by side, but Viktor rarely uttered a word. They worked in strange silence— Elias thought it would be best to keep his words and thoughts to himself. He worked hard and did what Viktor told him to do, but when Elias thought nobody was watching, he popped a few grapes in his mouth.

Saba, a plump, skittish man was working nearby. He was snooping on Elias and spoke up. "Uh oh! Don't let Viktor, see you do that. Oh no, oh please don't do that again."

"*What?* Look at all these grapes that fall to the floor. What's his problem?" Elias spoke up.

"Uh oh, I tell you this for your own good. Don't get noticed by Viktor."

Hearing Saba, Viktor looked their way and rambled over to them.

"What are you too squawking about?" Viktor said and glared at Saba and continued. "Yes, my good man, I saw the boy eat the grapes. What do you think I would do to him, huh? Who do you think I am? Some kind of beast?"

"Oh, oh! No sir," Saba stuttered.

"Don't call me sir—just call me Viktor. And for you," he poked out his chin looking at Elias and said, "what's that thing hanging around your neck?

"It's, it's just an amulet—for—good luck. Yes, for good luck."

"Well isn't that nice. See my *amulet* around my neck? Viktor stuck his neck out and pulled down his collar showing his scares.

"Yes." Elias sheepishly said.

"THAT'S for good luck." Viktor said and walked away.

Elias looked over at Saba who was trembling and said, "What a grouch."

"Oh, oh, just don't mess with him."

"Don't worry. I'm on my way out of here soon."

After Elias cleaned the floor around the presses, Viktor demanded that he rake and clean the stables. Elias did what Viktor told him to do and bit his tongue rather than question the man's instructions. He reminded himself that this was a mere stop in his travels as the omens he witnessed were leading him this very way. He needed food and money and a day of work would give him both. *I'll just do what he tells me to do. I'm on my way out of here soon*, he thought.

Hours later, the cellar master told Viktor and Elias it was quitting time. In silence, Elias followed Viktor and the other men to the workers' quarters, where they rested before the supper bell. The aromas from the cook's kettles rode lightly on the air, masking the strong body odor of the men in their confined quarters.

After supper, the men lined up to receive their daily pay. Because of his status as a novice, they shoved Elias to the back of the line. *This is a necessary evil,* he thought. *I need food and money and I'll be on my way,* he kept telling himself, but he didn't know how long he could keep his thoughts and actions to himself.

TEN

First Fear

Little more than a place to keep the sun and rain away, the workers' quarters were large and could sleep a dozen boys and men in bunks made of old mattresses with worn and dirty linens. Basic in all ways, these structures had no running water. A few kerosene lanterns worked overtime to illuminate the room at night. A table or two rounded out the amenities. There were two such quarters tucked off the beaten path with a well between them. The men were free to drink and wash in this common area.

As the last rays of the sun shone through the small windows of quarters number two, some of the men were already asleep, while others sat outside smoking and enjoying the infrequent breezes that wafted from the vineyard and weaved their way through the camp.

Janos' home was about one hundred paces west, with a stonewall that drew the line between him and the workers. There was an unspoken rule that kept all in their places.

It was hot and stuffy in the quarters, so Elias pulled off his shirt, and he sprawled on a bottom bunk. The amulet never left his neck and laid squarely on his chest. He used his knapsack to prop up his head and covered it with a pillow that he found on the bed.

He assumed no one would bother him, so he spent the time sketching. His sword rested between him and the wall but he covered it with a blanket. As Elias positioned himself as he sketched, he disturbed the sword's covering and he was unaware this made the handle visible. Cimbora was half-asleep at the foot of his bunk. It was quiet, and only a few other men were sleeping.

Moments later, Viktor lumbered through the door and approached Elias' bunk. He hunched over so their heads were at an even height, and their eyes met, which made Elias uneasy. Elias felt Viktor's breath, and it was strangely hot and stunk like rotting fish. Disgusted at the sudden situation, Elias kept his eyes set on Viktor's eyes. They were black as pitch.

"So, Elias, what are you are doing?"

"Ah, nothing," he said as he slipped his sketchbook out of sight with his right hand.

"Just what I thought."

As Elias skillfully tucked the sketchbook away, Viktor's attention turned to the handle of the sword.

"What's that?" Viktor asked pointing to the partially hidden sword.

"It's nothing, really, nothing," Elias, said stammering.

"Nothing? I have eyes, chump. You've noticed my eyes, *haven't you?*"

"Yes. Yes, I've noticed them."

"So what is it? Looks like *something* to me," Viktor was angry but soft-spoken.

"It's just something I'm taking to someone. That's all," Elias said nervously.

"Well, it has the same mark on it that YOU have around your neck. Funny, isn't it? "

Elias said nothing in return. The moment seemed as if it would never end and he felt tiny beads of sweat break out over his scalp. His throat tightened. Viktor stood up and slowly began to walk away. Elias sighed but Viktor paused and turned to Elias.

"Boy," Viktor commanded, "how about you join us out back for a game of cards?"

"Thanks, but not tonight," Elias said with some sudden confidence.

"I'm sorry? Maybe you didn't hear me," Viktor retorted with a hint of anger.

"Ah, okay," said Elias unable to believe this turn of events.

"Be around back in ten minutes."

Viktor slithered out the door laughing. Elias scurried to put on his shirt and to conceal the handle of the sword. Cimbora nudged his way closer to Elias, sitting next to him with a paw on the hidden sword, giving Elias assurance that his belongings would be safe. Cimbora turned his large head to Elias and dug his snout into the boy's ribs, showing deep affection for his friend. This made Elias smile.

"Okay, boy, be back soon. Come look for me if it gets too late."

*****

Elias followed the sounds of haughty laughter and the flicker of torches. He stumbled over exposed roots and rocks along the way, sensing this was an omen. He heard the fluttering bats in the trees as a stiff cool breeze came from nowhere. He slowed his pace as he approached the group of men. He watched them from afar as the men surrendered to Viktor's every utterance.

"Oh…oh, I see the boy has arrived…just in time," Saba stammered.

"So he showed up. Welcome, Elias," Viktor said with a disturbing politeness. He was pleased to see Elias was alone and empty-handed.

There were four men huddled around a makeshift table playing cards and swigging stolen wine. Elias remembered most of them from supper, including Saba, who seemed out of place with this group.

"Pass the flagon of wine to Elias," Viktor commanded Saba.

As if he were Viktor's servant, Saba passed Elias the container. He gave Elias a faint but troubled grin.

"Where did you get this? Is this stolen wine?" Elias asked the men.

Immediate laughter from the gang erupted but their amusement ended when Viktor started his outburst.

"Listen, boy, I steal nothing. Do you understand?

I borrow. What I can take is mine. Now drink!" He said with an abrupt spike in his voice.

Elias took the large container with his left hand and drank.

"I've noticed you're left-handed," said Viktor, "You know that's the hand of Ordak—the evil one himself?"

"I don't know *your* Ordak. He probably uses his feet to wash his face…you know nothing of me."

"I've heard enough of this," said Saba, "It's time to play cards. Don't you agree? It's time we all play cards. Well, isn't it," he said as his words tapered off.

"Well, well, Saba, if you say so," Viktor said, patronizing him.

The men played several games and drank from the same flagon, only replenishing it from time to time from the stolen cask. As they passed the container, Elias only pretended to drink the wine as the dark of the night and the shared ceramic flagon schemed to keep his ways secret.

As the night grew, so did the raucous laughter. The men were drunk. One man slumped over the table and passed out. Another man folded his cards and quit but continued drinking, leaving Viktor, Saba, and Elias.

"Now, let's up the ante. Let's play for something real. How about we play for that shiny amulet around your neck," Viktor offered.

Elias could not believe his ears but acted with indifference.

"And what will you put up?" Elias boldly asked both men.

"I'm out. I don't have anything you want, Viktor," Saba cried.

"So it's me and you, Elias. So what should I wager? I know, if you lose, I get the amulet. If I lose, I will not tell Janos who stole the wine," Viktor said with a sinister laugh.

"That's not fair!"

"Fair? What is fair? Are you naïve enough to think that life is fair?"

"Well, no, I'm not. But what do playing cards have to do with life?"

"Everything! It has *everything* to do with life. It *is* about luck, skill and rules, not to mention choices. It's about my life and yours. You see, if you really want to know, you are looking at your own reflection when you look at me."

"What…what are you talking about?" Elias nervously licked his dry lips.

"You don't get it, Elias, do you? Do you think I grew up wanting to slave ten-hour days making someone else rich? I work hard, for what? To line the pockets of someone else! Do you think I grew up to be the man you see here tonight?"

"You're still a young man and capable of doing anything you want."

"Ha! Don't make me laugh. See Elias, it *is* too late. Who I am has been sucked from my soul." Viktor looked down and was pensive. Elias felt a trace of pity for Viktor. He reached up to his amulet and pressed it against his chest. Saba, sitting off to one side, was dumbfounded at what transpired. He quietly and deliberately watched as the events unfolded, wisely staying silent.

Although Nattymama had given Elias the amulet, it was just a mere piece of metal. *What is all the fuss over this symbol?* Elias thought while he deciphered his avalanche of emotions. *I could give him this thing and be done with it—done with Viktor.*

"Viktor."

"Yes, Elias," Viktor raised his head and responded in a tone which tried to draw out Elias' words.

"I can…what I mean is, you can have…"

"NO!" Saba screamed in horror.

"Are you mad?" shouted Viktor.

"Run, Elias, run," warned Saba.

Stunned, Elias stood up and froze. Viktor leapt toward Saba and struck him with the back of his fist, and Saba fell face first to the wine-drenched ground. Motionless, he lay moaning as blood streamed from his gashed cheek. Viktor then turned to Elias with only the table between the two. He glared at him but spoke calmly.

"Now for you. If you give me the amulet, I will let you walk away a free man…ah, *boy*."

Elias assumed he was no match for Viktor but now innately understood the amulet must be more than just an old keepsake that Nattymama stowed away for nostalgic reasons. Maybe it *did* have powers.

"I'll give it to you if you tell me why. Why do you want it?" Elias responded calmly.

Viktor erupted angrily, "Just give it to me. Give-it-to-me."

Viktor began to step towards Elias, reaching out his hand. Unexpectedly Elias flipped up the table on its end, buying some time with a temporary barricade. Regaining his composure, only Elias noticed Cimbora as he quietly approached the area. He gripped the sword in his teeth.

Elias then witnessed something so bizarre that he couldn't believe what he was seeing. Viktor stopped ten paces in front of Elias and from deep inside let out a peculiar but mad bellow. Then it happened. His arms and legs stretched as if he were made of clay. His misshapen limbs were grotesque. His feet and hands evolved to hideous claws. Now hunched over, out of his back sprang large bat-like wings. His skin turned to lizard scales, but the changes yet to come were the most disturbing part of this sick event. His neck grew three feet in length and his head contorted and transfigured itself to that of a snake. His head looked like a cobra's head—and a gigantic one at that. Disgustingly, two additional necks emerged from his shoulders, each with a similar serpent head.

Viktor's inner self was now on display. Paralyzed by this scary and monstrous transformation, the beast put him in a trance. Viktor was a Sarkany! The same strange being that Nattymama had described stood before him that he was sure it was a creature from her imagination. Elias had a half a moment to decide to run or defend himself.

The beast lunged at him, knocking him down with a swift blow from his revolting arm thrashing him squarely across his jaw. In a haze, Elias collapsed to the ground like a house of cards. The Sarkany stood over Elias, straddling him. It whipped one of its reptile heads down to Elias' face. Its breath was stinky and hot, but this act revived Elias from his semi-conscious state.

Its small lizard nostrils flared, but Elias locked his attention on his eyes. His eyes were unchanged. They were Viktor's—the transfiguration had left his eyes untouched. The Sarkany gazed directly into Elias' eyes. Looking at the repugnant face and into its eyes, Elias saw into Viktor's soul, and what he saw beneath his dark and murky surface was empty.

"This is your fate, Elias. When you imprison your own nature, you become barren. You become something you loathe. We all loathe something in us. Some of the paths we follow don't always lead us to something better. We can lose our way, and those mazes lead to an end, not a beginning."

Elias began to move, but the Sarkany stomped on his left wrist, sending excruciating pain throughout his arm. Elias jerked his head back and forth and only then, out of the corner of his eye, he saw his companion inching forward, bearing his sword. The Sarkany did not detect Cimbora's advance.

"Elias, you are like me. Good for nothing. Mediocrity pleases Ordak. Ordak will embrace you as he has me. I can now take the shape of humans and escort them to the throne of Ordak. It is an honor."

"I don't care about Ordak," Elias said struggling to try to get free.

"You are no match for the evils that are buried beneath your bones that pierce your heart," the Sarkany said unleashing an evil laughter. "When you betray yourself, who is it that will help you?"

At that moment, Cimbora came from behind carrying the sword. He placed it near Elias' right hand and out of sight of the Sarkany. Elias slowly and quietly stretched out his arm to reach the blade as the Sarkany fixed his eyes on his. Elias guardedly wrapped each finger around its leather grip. At the touch, he felt an adrenaline rush come over him. Now every second seemed like three, giving him a keenly sharpened thought process. He knew what he needed to do. He *felt* what he should do.

With all the might he could muster, he swiftly hurled the sword upward, striking the Sarkany's bony back. The beast raised his head in pain and let out an inhuman and terrifying scream. With blood pouring from his back, he fell forward, allowing Elias to free himself. Elias scrambled to his feet. The Sarkany quickly rebounded and turned to face him.

"I know you've never wielded a sword, so I allowed you one lucky blow. Without that wretched dog, you would be ready to follow me. Don't worry, I can rip that amulet from your scrawny neck before you can raise your weapon."

With that, the Sarkany charged toward Elias. Still stunned from the experience but focused, Elias knew what he needed to do. With both hands, as if he was harvesting wheat with a sickle, he held the sword to one side and, pointing it to the ground, stood motionless. Furiously the Sarkany advanced toward him. With the faint light of only the full moon, Elias looked into its eyes one last time. The Sarkany spat fire, and as it closed in, Elias, with a swift and precise upward swing, sliced through one of the three necks. His stroke cleanly delivered the serpent's head to the muddy ground. The Sarkany stumbled and dropped to its knees. Elias, not knowing what to expect, stood paralyzed.

Alive but disoriented, the Sarkany managed to stand, but with an impulsive and erratic movement, it retreated, turning to run in the opposite direction. It fled from the camp, flapping its spindly wings and awkwardly lifting its bony body into the air. With one last screech, it was gone.

There on the ground, the serpent's head magically transformed back to the likeness of Viktor's head. As Elias looked on with disbelief, the grotesque head turned to stone. Elias stood, dripping with sweat, and released each finger, one at a time, from the hilt of the sword. The blade clanged to the ground where the Sarkany had once stood. He rubbed his left wrist and made sure it was not broken. Spent and weary, he stumbled to where Cimbora and Saba sat. Tasting his own blood, he grabbed the flagon of wine and drank several long gulps. He turned to Saba.

"Did you know about Viktor?"

"Yes … ah … yes, I did," he stammered. Taking a deep breath, he continued, "But that was not Viktor."

"What? Are you crazy?"

"Oh *no*. Viktor is somewhere else tonight. Perhaps in his bunk or gone into a nearby village. It just might be that you never met Viktor. That's why these Sarkanys are wily. They take on the likeness of others. Why, some might even be someone we trust."

"Why, then, did you wait so long to warn me? I could have been killed!"

"I THOUGHT he was coming for me tonight. He told me to say nothing or I'd never speak again," Saba said turning his head.

Calmly Elias paused and looked down to his chest, and asked, "Why did he want this amulet?"

"Because *you* have it, and he *doesn't*. Please remember, my young friend, that he still wants it."

ELEVEN

One Song

Hidden in the silver clouds, the sun seemed nonexistent. Earth turned cold. A mist hung like a fine veil and a pall emanated from all things. Elias awoke in his bunk. There was an uneasy stillness as he found most of the men were already up, dressed, and gone to breakfast. He sat up in his bed and scratched his head, wondering if what he had experienced had all just been a nightmare. He swung his legs to the side of the bed, planted his bare feet on the floor, and reached down to pet Cimbora.

Janos walked through the door. Expressionless he said nothing and sat next to Elias on the bunk. With a slight smile, he looked kindly at Elias. He nodded as if he were trying to tell him something without uttering so much as a word. With a gulp, he finally spoke.

"You know, you are a fine young man. I like you, but it is time you moved on, Elias. I will give you another day's earnings and some food to take with you, but it is time. Yesterday I met you as a boy and today…"

"So you heard about last night?"

"I did."

"Is that why you have come to me this morning—to send me on my way?"

"Yes, it is. Viktor, or rather, the Sarkany, was waiting for you and the longer you stay, the better the chances are that it will come back."

"I guess you're right."

"See, in this forest, we've come to expect unusual happenings and peculiar beings, but it doesn't mean I want them in my camp. Do you understand me?"

"I understand," said Elias.

With a pleasant chuckle, Janos went on to say, "I suspect you will find a difference in yourself. It is not every night a boy looks squarely into the eyes of a Sarkany. You have something to tell your children one day."

"Yes, sir, I guess I do."

"But, you know Elias, I am old and sorry to say I have seen my fair share of beasts like the one you encountered last night. I know about the Sarkany and they are what they are. Elias, I do not want more than we can handle around here. You understand?"

Elias nodded and agreed with the old man. He thought about asking Janos more about the Sarkany but decided to keep his thoughts to himself.

"You're a good man, Elias. I will give you food, water and some money and you should leave this morning. For your sake, I hope you find in your heart what it is you are looking for."

With that, Janos pointed to the amulet, offered a halfhearted smile, and walked away.

*****

The new day's mist evaporated in the glow of the rising sun. Elias and Cimbora left the workers' quarters and kept their eyes looking forward. They took the only clear path deeper into the woods. As they walked, Elias desperately tried to wipe away the sights and scenes from the nightmare he had lived only a few short hours earlier. Although he hadn't believed her at the time, Nattymama had been right all along in her descriptions and warnings about what he might encounter in the forest. *She knows her stuff.*

Looking overhead, Elias rediscovered the Turul

from a day earlier as it was gliding in and out of sight due to the boughs that were nearly touching the wispy, misshapen clouds. This gave him the sense that all was okay. As they traveled down the path, Cimbora frequently trotted ahead but was never out of Elias' sight. They journeyed deeper into the green forest.

Elias' loosely strapped his sword to the outside of his knapsack, and he felt it swing back and forth in cadence with each step. With his right hand, he reached behind his shoulder and touched the hilt, grabbed it, and pulled it upward and out of the knot. Without breaking his stride, he examined the blade. In the sun's rays that teemed through the thick branches and dense leaves, the weapon shimmered like a cleaned and polished museum artifact. His troubled thoughts of his fearful night, like the fog earlier that morning, were disappearing in the brilliance of the late morning. He beamed.

"I'm not so bad with this thing, am I?" he asked looking down at Cimbora.

As he negotiated the crooked and overgrown path, he admired the lifeless piece of steel that, perhaps, saved his life. One thought led to another. *I am sure to find my fortune now*, he thought.

As the morning was turning to noon, Elias paused to rest by a stream. He pulled off his dusty boots, rolled up his pant legs, and waded into the cool water, as he liked to do. The tranquil stream that flowed from the neighboring mountains refreshed him. Cimbora lapped up a drink, stretched out on the bank and followed the slow advances of a praying mantis.

Stepping out of the stream and sitting on a nearby rock, Elias pulled out his sketchbook and looked at it blankly. He raised his chin and scratched his neck. He put the sketchbook to one side. *This can wait*, he thought. He lay back, placing his hands behind his head, and closed his eyes. An instant later, he fell asleep.

After what seemed to be only a minute or two, Elias awoke to a beautiful sound. Sitting up and rubbing his eyes, he looked from side to side trying to determine from where the music was coming. It was faintly sweet and drifted by him on a soft breeze. It stirred his curiosity. Remembering Nattymama, as she occasionally played stringed instruments, Elias thought what he heard must be a lute. Joining the music was a man singing. He pulled on his boots and, as he did so, his sketchbook slid off the rock and out of sight without his noticing. Gathering most of his possessions, he put his knapsack over one arm and carried the sword. He and Cimbora started toward the lilt of the music.

As they continued down another path, the voice they heard was more audible and enchanting.

"We've got to find where this is coming from, boy."

Elias suddenly froze in his tracks. He looked from side to side, trying to hone in on what he heard. Figuring out where it was coming from, Elias left the path and walked further into the woods, stepping high over the tall grasses and skirting the thorny shrubs. As he drew closer to where the music was coming from, he was amazed at what was before him.

Playing the lute and singing in absolute splendor was a rather large and hideous man sitting on a fallen tree. The man was obese and hunched over. He had a mangled nose and one eye drooped lower than the other. Clumps of hair grew from his head, but the sounds that came from his mouth and fingertips were angelic.

The man saw Elias but continued his song. He

nodded, as if to invite him to come closer. Elias sat on the ground mesmerized by him. The musician came to the end of the piece he was playing and gently placed the lute to his side. He brought his hands together in a prayerful fashion and looked at Elias.

"That was absolutely beautiful, sir. My name is Elias."

"Thank you. No one's ever called me that – *sir*, I mean my name is Lantos."

"Where did you learn to sing and play like that?"

"Many years ago. So long ago it feels as if I have always sung and played." Looking directly at Elias, he cocked his head to one side and said, "You are wearing the amulet."

"So everyone keeps telling me about it. What's so special about it?" he asked shaking his head.

"I've seen many come this way wearing that exact amulet," he said with concern and then, giving Elias a smile, he asked, "So, is it true that it has powers?"

"I don't know. It's hard to tell." He looked down to his sword and said, "Maybe the magic is in this shiny blade." He held the sword close to his face seeing his reflection and proudly examining the cold steel. "I'm not convinced I really need this amulet. I've got this…" He paused and looked at Lantos. Before he thought about what he was doing he asked, "Do you want it?" and held out the amulet to the lutist.

"Heavens, no! I'm smart enough to know that is *yours*."

Sniffing the ground, Cimbora mooched over to Lantos, and plopped at his feet. He looked up at him, and let out a friendly bark. They laughed and Lantos reached down his large but amazingly gentle hand and delicately scratched behind Cimbora's ears. "What a beautiful dog you are! You have a large head, too." The two laughed. Enjoying the moment, Elias picked up the lute and handed it to his new friend."

"Please play some more."

Lantos smiled, nodded, positioned the lute on his lap, and began to play and sing the same song. Elias sat back and enjoyed what he heard. When he finished, Elias respectfully asked Lantos to play something else.

"I am very sorry to disappoint you…"

"What do you mean?"

"I know but one song."

Elias was baffled. He'd never heard of anyone with such natural skill and talent who only knew one song!

"I sit here every day and play the lute and sing my song. Elias, if it helps you to understand, I am no longer from your world. I live here in this magical forest."

Elias sat up and leaned forward. "Tell me Lantos, why do you have this existence now?"

"I live in seclusion. My house is up a ways." He pointed toward the mountains.

"I left my home many years ago. I walked for miles—until I could go no further and here I am. I learned to take care of all my needs out here. I discovered that nobody judges me out here."

"Lantos, what do you mean? You should learn more. You shouldn't care what others say or think. You have many songs to learn. You are running away!"

"Perhaps you are right." He paused and said, "So, if you don't mind me asking where are *you* going?"

"Um, good point. I guess you could say I'm running away to find something—my fortune."

"Me too. My *song*, perhaps, is my fortune. I call it my answer. It brings me joy and if that's all I have, it's enough for me.

"Lantos, I don't understand."

"It's simple. Let me explain. I repulsed all who saw me including my mama and papa! They thought my life should be that of someone who stays out of sight and performs duties that no one else cares to do. I grew up cleaning stoves and chimneys. As this is a dirty job, I did it when no one was home."

"Yeah, but what does that have to do with your talents?"

"I'm getting to that…one day as I worked, I sang the song you just heard. The owner of the house walked in on me and, like you, was very surprised but pleased. He played the lute as I sang and later taught me to play. I told my parents and even sang and played for them. On his dying day, the good man gave me his lute. I've cherished it ever since."

"So? What did they say? They must have been so proud and happy to hear you."

Lantos laughed quietly but without warning, he became sullen. Tears streamed down his face. "No, they were not proud. My *parents* said they were happy I had *one* song in me but told me to put my dream away.

Elias interrupted Lantos, angry on his behalf and said, "What are you talking about? Put your dream away? Were they deaf?"

"No, my young friend, they were not deaf. They could hear just fine. They told me that nobody would teach, or even listen to me, if they had to see my face."

As bitter a statement as that was, Lantos had a warm, kind heart. With a quivering lip, a tear ran down Elias' face…and then another. Elias looked skyward and saw the Turul perched on a branch above his head. She spread her wings taking to flight and rode a current.

*****

Later that day, long after he had said good-bye to Lantos, Elias and Cimbora walked along a path that headed west. Elias' mind wandered. He looked up and realized he had not seen the Turul for some time. Doubting there was any significance to its disappearance, Elias began to think about Lantos and how his one song not only brought the musician joy, but also stirred something deep within his own heart. His story had hit home. *He has a talent to share…couldn't they see that? It is clear as day.*

He contemplated and reflected on the chance meeting. Thinking about him, Elias was surprised to discover that he couldn't remember exactly what Lantos looked like—the only thing that stood out was the beauty the lute player brought to his day, and beauty of the lute player.

TWELVE

Wall

With Cimbora by his side and focused on the path before him, Elias trudged on in silence. Brittle twigs and brown leaves crunched beneath their feet with every other step.

"Boy, I wish I knew where we were headed…I mean I know my answers are somewhere out there, but without the Turul as a guide, I'm not so sure we're headed the right way," Elias said as he abruptly stopped in his tracks and looked in all directions.

Cimbora trotted onward, paused and crooked his neck looking back at Elias. Panting, he let out a gentle bark ending with a fade as if he was asking a question. Elias beamed from ear to ear at his friend and he resumed the journey. As they continued, Elias detected the murmur of the subtle movement of a river in the distance. Altering his course, he followed the soothing and inviting sounds.

"Cimbora, how about we take a break and fill

up the canteen?" he asked bending down to rub Cimbora's side with several long strokes. "You're a good boy—always around when I need you. Hope I'm there for you too."

It was at that moment that from nowhere, Elias spotted a man. He was excavating large stones from the river. The man wasn't too far downstream from them. He was knee deep in the briskly flowing water. Considering the load of stone in the man's dilapidated wagon just on the riverbank, he must have been unearthing rock for the better part of the day.

Probably twice Elias' age, the man was rather tall and had a bushy mustache. Beads of sweat glistened on his shiny face and arms. Clearly, his modeled and rough hands were filthy and calloused.

Rustling flimsy tree limbs as they walked near to make extra noise as not to frighten the man, Elias was curious but sensed he should be cautious. As Elias drew closer, the man raised his head slightly and acknowledged him with a forced, closed mouth smile and a nod but kept about his tiring, backbreaking business. Without so much as a word, he bent at the waist, and with a rusty and dented up trowel, continued digging stones from the firm grip of the earth. Removing them from the water one at a time, he examined them carefully before making the decision whether to gently toss them in his wagon or leave them off to the side. By the looks of it, Elias noticed the man was quite selective. He would close one eye, twist his puckered lips and tilt his head examining each as if it was a rare gem.

By this time, Elias had filled the canteen and he and Cimbora were relaxing on the bank. A touch amused, Elias was captivated at the man's actions, as he was so precise and calculated with his actions.

"What are you going to do with all of those stones?"

The man stopped his arduous task and stood straight; he placed his left hand on the small of his back and stretched to ease his aching muscles. First eyeballing Elias up and down, he paused, and then did the same to Cimbora. Without a word, he pulled out a bandana, wiped his forehead, and blew his nose. Elias tightened his smile and exhaled with a short shake of his head.

"Well, I can see this isn't going anywhere...nice

meeting you, I guess, but we ought to be on our way. C'mon Cimbora, let's head out of here."

"You talking about those stones?" the man asked pointing to his wagon.

"Ah, yeah. What are you going to do with all those?" Elias asked again.

"Well, I gather them for my papa," huffed the man.

"I see. So what is your papa building?"

"A wall. Yes sir, a big wall. We've been building it for as long as I can remember. My papa owns a hundred or so acres of farmland, and it is my job to collect these stones and build a six-foot wall around the property. It's an important job."

"It is? Why is that?"

"Papa's told me so, you see?" the man said.

"Oh. He told you so. Yes, I see," said Elias.

"He told me that walls solve lots of problems. See, one day the land will be mine and no one should dispute its boundaries, and no one in their right mind COULD dispute them with the wall. No one can come take away what is rightfully ours. You gotta watch for that. These stones make it clear. They keep others in their place. They do—really, they do," said the man.

"Do you have trespassers coming in and taking your harvest? I mean, if you're still building that wall, seems like you've got folks coming in everyday making mischief. You convinced me that without that wall, you're sitting ducks," Elias said chuckling under his breath.

"No one is taking our harvest, but when some folks trespass—and that's what they are doing—we put them to work for us. They seem fine with that. That's what most of them want—to work—and if they work hard we give them food and a place to live. As long as they keep up their end of the bargain, we're okay with them."

"Sounds like your papa has it all figured out," Elias said with sarcasm.

"Don't tell them, but they do the work most folks around here don't want to do any way. They're the folks that don't have powers," the man went on to say.

"I see…having no powers in this place does put you at a disadvantage, I can tell you that," said Elias.

"Then you know what I'm saying?" asked the

man.

"Not exactly, but let me ask you this, does anyone dispute the boundaries now?" asked Elias.

"Well…no, they don't. People around here know what is ours."

"So you've been collecting stones, hauling them home and building a wall your entire life?" Elias asked.

"Yes, that's right," said the man.

Growing agitated with Elias, the man turned away and continued to hunt for stones in silence. Elias shook his head, looked down at Cimbora, and smiled halfheartedly. He didn't know what to think at that moment.

Squatting down to scratch Cimbora behind his floppy ears, Elias said under his breath, "If I were to make a guess, Cimbora, he's already finished that wall. Come on, boy let's get out of here."

The two began to walk away without saying anything else to the strange man. They heard only the clang and clatter of stones thrust on stones.

Having gone only ten paces, the man yelled out, "I heard that!"

Elias felt embarrassed and turned to the man

and said, "I didn't mean any harm by what I said. I just don't get why you're doing what you're doing and why it's important. I mean, if you spend your life always worried about what might happen and you build a wall with all the good days of your life, what do you get from that? I think it just keeps you locked up and those you might meet, locked out. I think that can only make a person look on the dark side of things," said Elias.

Annoyed, the man asked, "What makes you so smart?"

"I'm not 'so smart', but I know what walls do and if you think about it, you know what I'm saying."

After an uncomfortable and unnaturally drawn out pause, the man blurted out, "My name is Vilmos. How about you?"

"I'm Elias and this is my friend Cimbora."

"It's late. You and Cimbora can come back with me to the farm and get something to eat and have a place to rest your head for the night."

*****

Because of the many irregular sized platters heaped high with meats, bowls overflowing with vegetables and bottles of ciders and wine, Elias could not see the surface of the table. The aroma of the mixture of ghastly concoctions was unappetizing at best. Dimly lighted, the room was full of candles and torches attached to the musty walls. Elias sat between Vilmos and his father sitting at opposite ends of the narrow table while Cimbora lay at Elias feet sleeping.

"Elias…it is Elias, is it not?" Vilmos' father asked as Elias nodded his head. "You are going someplace? Where?"

"I've got someone to see. That's all."

"Someone to see?" roared the grotesque man spewing morsels of chewed food with every word. "You see me and Vilmos. Who else would you want to see?" he asked and continued without waiting for Elias to answer. "I see what is around your neck…it is an amulet. Hmmm, I know about such things… I see you carry a sword too," the man said spearing his mutton.

Elias looked up at the man and then to the corner where his sword and other belongings rested on a stool. He felt his heart beat faster and his hands began to feel clammy.

"Let me ask you again, my good boy. Where are you going?" he asked, struggling to lean toward Elias.

Elias sat up straight. He looked at the old man and then Vilmos to answer. "I'm seeking answers, and it isn't any of your business."

"I see. So you think you must leave your home, wherever that is, carry a sword and search the world over to find ANSWERS? Let me tell you a thing or two my skinny friend; first, we live comfortably on our land. Secondly, we have what we need, and we protect ourselves from all those who want to suck out our very soul. You my friend, perhaps you are a pleasant young man, but appearances can be deceiving. You must be 'one of those.'"

"One of those?" exclaimed Elias. "What are you talking about?"

"Nothing is good enough for you—huh? You search and search, but you will never find what it is you are looking for." He said looking at Vilmos and then continued. "Yes Vilmos? You'd agree with me—YES."

"Of...of course, Papa," stuttered Vilmos.

"Pardon me," Elias interrupted, "but that's what you think—not me."

Changing his tone, the man said, "So who is this good soul who you think will help you? Pass the platter of mutton and liver… and the bread, too, while you're at it."

Elias swallowed hard, with two hands picked up the unwieldy platter of nasty food, and passed the dish to the host. "I'm looking for Zoltan."

The man contorted his face upon his answer as he violently stabbed the steaming meat. "I've heard of this Zoltan. I've heard of his ways. As a matter of fact, you have confirmed my guess and because of this, you have disrupted my dinner." He said with a growing disdain. He then extended his arms out to either side as Elias sat in awe wondering what the man was doing.

"Papa, no! Don't do this. He's my guest and I invited him home for a meal and a place to sleep. He will be gone by morning."

Elias spoke up, "What is going on? He jumped to his feet but couldn't budge. His feet were rooted to the floor. With his arms still extended, the old man said something in a language that didn't seem human. Weird belches and burps filtered in and out of each sentence. The man repeated the same phrase and Cimbora lunged at the man. As he did, from the cracks in the floor a glistening brown strand that looked like the root of a tree sped toward Cimbora and wrapped itself around his legs and snout like a muzzle.

From under Elias, a dozen root-like projections emerged and imprisoned him where he stood. The room appeared to be turning in circles and the man's face came in and out of focus. With the roots propping him up, Elias lost consciousness.

"Vilmos, take these two to the crypt as I will take care of them later. I must finish my meal. Leave the amulet with him—I will have the joy of ripping it off his neck after I eat."

*****

Free of the roots that held him, Elias rested on the stone floor of a dark and dank cell. He opened his eyes only to see Cimbora sitting at his side. It was then that Vilmos entered through a small door. "Listen to me and I will show you the way out of here, but we need to act fast as Papa will be here soon."

"Thanks—I'm ready. I know when I'm not wanted. What was that all about?"

"It's a long story. But what you don't know is

that since you only saw him sitting at the table, you didn't see that when he began his incantation, the trunk of his body turned into... well, it turned into the trunk of a tree. He must use a special wheeled device to move around when this happens. It takes a day for him to change back."

Elias couldn't believe what he was hearing but didn't question it. "Too weird, but why should I trust you anyway? You brought us here knowing your papa is a...is a... whatever he is," exclaimed Elias. "I'll never look at trees the same way again."

"I'm sorry, but I haven't seen him like that in a long time. In fact, I thought he had changed for good. That's why I thought it was safe for you."

"Obviously not. How did I set him off?"

"It has to do with Zoltan and not really you. Let's just say that my papa's branch of the Tree of Life is bit rotten."

"Huh? Tree of Life? Do you mean THE Tree of Life?"

"You don't have the time for a long explanation right now. We know of Zoltan and we have seen travelers come this way searching for him. You must understand, we come from a place that has walls—and roots—and we do not understand what is beyond them."

"What? We met beyond these walls."

"This place you have journeyed to, although you cannot see it, is surrounded by walls and roots. Do you think your family or friends can find this place? Do you think you can leave this place unless you find your answers? Do you see where I'm coming from? You must continue your quest at once or you may settle for what's inside the walls if you know what I mean."

"I don't know why, but I trust you are telling me the truth," said Elias looking at Cimbora for a clue. Feeling reassured by the wag of Cimbora's tail, Elias said, "So how do we get out of here?"

"Go, at once, through that open door on the opposite side of where I entered—you cannot see it, but it will be there when you approach it. You merely have to believe there is a way out. When you go through it, you will see that I have placed your belongings and your sword on the other side. Keep going straight and you will see the sun rising. Go that way."

"Won't you come with us? This is no place for someone like you."

"No, I have another path I need to take, but I'm not ready."

THIRTEEN

Second Fear

Elias and Cimbora came to a clearing in the dense and dark forest. Looking to the sky, they were happy to see the Turul gliding in a huge circle. They followed her up and down a few hills before the great bird disappeared into the clouds. Spotting a small stream further down the path, Elias decided to use it as his guide. Hiking for another hour in silence, he grew tired. The sun was now hanging low on the horizon and he knew it was time to set up camp.

Breaking the silence, he heard sobbing that seemed to come from close by. Elias cautiously followed the cry down a crooked path. He stopped in his tracks, as he was unable to believe his eyes. About fifty paces ahead, he saw the back of an old woman wearing a long black cape and a hood that covered her head. She was sitting on a tree stump with a small campfire nearby. He took short steps as he approached, as he didn't know what to expect. He called out first, not wanting to startle her. "Hello…are you alright? Can…can I help you?" he asked with apprehension.

The old woman said nothing and wept even louder. Elias, only an arm's length away, leaned toward her. She peeled her bony hands from her face and raised her chin. Their eyes met and they both gasped.

"*Nattymama?*" Elias shouted.

"*Elias?* It *is* you! I found you," she shouted as she wiped her eyes.

They hugged and she kissed him on his cheek. Elias looked at her and gave her a smile.

"What are you doing out here, Nattymama?"

"I'm looking for you, of course."

"Me? Why?"

She looked down and rubbed her hands together. Taking her time to answer, she peeked up at Elias and gave him a smile in a manner that always defused him. "I should have never sent you away. It is far too dangerous."

"It *is* dangerous, but I can handle it. You told me what to expect. I've handled everything just fine."

"Yes, maybe so. But when I told your mama and papa, they were furious and threatened never to speak to me again—to banish me from the family. They told me I was mad for telling you such things. You may not know this, but that's why I live alone in my bungalow. Your papa thinks I am no good for you and the other children. He wants me at a distance, but NOW he wants me gone. I cannot have that. NO, I told them I would find you and bring you home."

"They let you travel here by yourself? That doesn't sound like Mama and Papa. They wouldn't let any harm come to you, no matter how angry they were. How did you get here?" asked Elias.

"NO—I would NEVER be that stupid. My dear friend, Mr. Varga who owns the apothecary, offered to accompany me out here to find you. He's good to me, and I know he's good to you, dear boy. He's collecting kindling as we speak just over that hill. Dear man, he is," she said raising her fingers to her lips.

"Nattymama, I still don't understand. You never just *change* your mind especially about things like this. I mean, this is big."

"Big—*shmig*. You cannot be out here and that's all there is to it. It is too dangerous, and I fear for you. Until your mama and papa shook some sense in me, I had all but forgotten about this *place*," she said as her shoulders pointed up, and she peered in all directions.

"Too dangerous! WHAT? You knew how dangerous it was and prepared me for this…weird place," Elias gritted his teeth and shook with anger.

"Elias, I know what I told you, but I was wrong," she grumbled. I have a new plan. Yes, a much better one. You'll see but we must get home at once."

"So I shouldn't find my fortune? I shouldn't look for my answers? You think I'm wrong to follow my heart and you want me to be unhappy? All of a sudden I don't know who I'm talking to… can't believe it…you're saying I should be a farmer?"

"Hogwash! There's that petulance I always warn you about; I'm afraid for you, my dear boy. We will leave at dawn and that's that," she said wagging her finger at him.

He turned his back to her. With his sword tied to the outside of his knapsack, he jerked it off his back and glumly flung it near the fire. Walking toward it, he sat on a boulder and stared blankly into flames. *I don't know who to trust anymore—she's like the rest of the adults—no different.* Cimbora barked fiercely at Nattymama. His bark turned to a growl.

"Hush boy. That's Nattymama." Heeding his master, Cimbora quietly sat at his feet but kept his eyes focused on the boy's grandmother.

She slowly walked toward him and as she did, she opened the palm of her hand and said, "Perhaps, Elias, you should give me that amulet. I believe it can only stir up more trouble. Look at you! You are so angry...and hand over the sword too."

Elias sat in silence as Nattymama finished speaking. He was very confused by this conversation. *Why is she worried about the amulet...and my sword? Has she lost it just like the townsfolk say?*

Just at that moment, the Turul swooped in and landed on a nearby branch. Elias had never seen the great bird close up. He was pleased that she had decided to join them. Nattymama stopped in her tracks and she grew uneasy as the bird began to caw.

Elias spoke up, "Why do you think the Turul is squawking?"

"I don't know but I don't like it one bit," she said sourly.

"But Nattymama, you told me that we are safe

when she is around."

"I know I told you that, but I don't like that bird. She's good for nothing. She's not like any Turul I remember. She's from a bad lot, I tell you. Scat, go, we don't want you anymore." The Turul flew off to a distant branch but remained in sight.

Elias looked at Nattymama in astonishment as she moved to sit on a boulder opposite of him. Mystified by all her actions, Elias remained quiet but mulled over the events of last few minutes.

"So, my boy, how about you take off that amulet and hand it to me? Do as I say, boy."

Elias sat up and sparked by her unusual command, he leaned forward and smiled, "This old thing, Nattymama?" He pulled it away from his chest and looked down at it. Letting it fall back onto his chest, he patted it and looked into her eyes.

"Yes, dear boy. Please forgive my touchiness, as this has been a trying day for your Nattymama. So please give it to me."

"Why would you want something that I found in the muck of a ditch? It means nothing," Elias said.

"I wouldn't be so sure of that, Elias. Where

exactly did you find it?"

Elias hesitated no longer. Lunging for his sword he had flung away moments before, he swung the blade and swiftly and precisely severed her head right below her chin. Much to his relief, the body fell to the ground and, at once, transfigured to that of the Sarkany. Now it had only one head. The other gruesome head, which lay on the ground, morphed into that of a lizard serpent and became stone.

Slowly rising from the ground, the Sarkany, with two drooping and headless necks, unfolded its wings. It let out an inhuman groan and took to the air.

Elias thrust the point of the sword into the rocky soil with all his might before collapsing to the ground next to it. He fought back tears of horror and despair. He desperately tried to clear the nauseating vision from his memory, but he couldn't blot it out, as it seemed determined to linger.

The Turul swooped into the camp and perched herself on the hilt of the sword. Cimbora's big tongue lapped Elias' face. The boy opened his eyes and sat up. Looking at his companions, Elias muttered, "I *could* have been wrong...dead wrong.

FOURTEEN

Breaking the Spell

Another day and night passed. Elias was both repulsed and euphoric about his encounters and triumphs of the past week. He was feeling a little more hardened but also considerably more confident in himself. His mind wandered to the ideal life he was certain to live. He could not imagine that anything more treacherous or vile could possibly come his way. He knew deep inside that Zoltan would guide him to his fortune.

Elias and Cimbora traveled near the base of the mountain. Elias could hear water gushing and bubbling nearby, though he couldn't see it from where he was on the path. As he walked, the sound got louder. Before him, he saw a dozen gigantic cypress trees that were well over fifty meters high. They stood like Grecian pillars. They were a gateway to a spring that emitted steam from its sapphire waters.

"Cimbora, we must be near Budapest. That must be the thermal waters that Nattymama told me about when I was a little boy."

As he got closer, the steam became thicker, and the aroma was delicate and uplifting. He knelt down and let the water run between his fingers. As he touched it, he felt its warmth and healing powers. He cupped his hands and drank.

Wearing only his amulet and shorts, he carefully eased himself into the spring. Beginning with his toes, then legs, and finally to his chest, he felt the deep warmth of the frothing water. There were flat and jagged-edged rock formations that outlined the spa, so he had to be careful as he submerged himself. Keeping his arms below the bubbles, he felt for a place where he could sit and rest. Finding a smooth slab of stone formed from a million years of erosion, he leaned back against its even ledge. As the steam rose under his chin and up his cheeks, his eyelids became heavy. Fighting to keep them open, his eyelids gently closed.

Some time passed and Elias was half-asleep. Cimbora slept soundly as if under a spell, and he lay with his front paws in the water on the edge of the spring. Elias felt the soothing water bubble against his aching limbs and torso. He was content. His journey, so far, had been both a physical and mental one, and he still had the bruises and the scabs to show it. The steam circled in front of his face on a lone and slight breeze. As he inhaled the vapors, he felt an overwhelming peace. Opening his eyes for a second now and then, he could see very little through the warm fog.

Although the air became still, the nearby foliage rustled for just a moment. There was another rustle. The disturbance went undetected by Elias and Cimbora because of the churning and natural jets bubbling under the water. The sound was mesmerizing. Cimbora was now in a deep sleep. There was another rustle of the tall grasses nearby.

"Hellooooo," a feminine and lyrical voice called out.

Snapped back to reality, Elias sat up and reached for the amulet, making sure it was still hanging around his neck. He looked in all directions but could not tell where the voice was coming from.

"Hellooooo." He scratched his head. *There it is again.*

Bemused, he stammered, "Uh, hello? Where are you? Who's there?"

Through the curtain of steam, an enchanting face at water level came into full view.

"Hello," she smiled.

"Ah...stay there and don't come any closer. Stay under water—please," Elias blurted, feeling strangely uncomfortable.

"My name is Lia." She was petite and she pulled her long brown hair to one side exposing a small pointed ear. Her beautiful eyes sparkled.

Captivated by her glow, Elias' thoughts whirled in his head. *Certainly, she can't bring me any harm,* he thought.

"I bring good fortune," she said in a breathy whisper. "What is your name?"

"My...my name," he stammered, "is Elias... please, stay right there and don't come any closer."

"If that is what you wish, Elias. I like your name—Elias," she giggled.

"Thank you and, yes, that is what I wish. You shouldn't sneak up on people. Especially when they are sleeping in the water." He paused and sank down a little further. "I think that maybe I've been soaking too long. I'm beginning to feel..." Before he could finish his sentence, Lia immersed herself under the water. Elias' head darted back and forth. *Where did she go?* He felt oddly anxious. Abruptly, he heard her voice but could not see her.

"Hello, Elias. Come join me," she said in a musical tone.

"No, I don't think so." Elias remembered what Nattymama had told him about some creature she called Vadleany. It was coming back to him but was still fuzzy…he couldn't remember what kind of havoc this elf could stir up, no matter how hard he tried.

"Come with me and live in the woods. You will be happy here. We have everything one would ever want. We do not work. There is no work to do. There is only play. This is a land of fortune."

Elias began to feel woozy and couldn't think straight. He felt as though he was falling under a spell.

"What…what do you…what do you mean? This is a land of…land of fortune?" Elias asked.

"You heard me. Give up your journey and live with me and the other girls and boys of the forest. We have no cares or problems."

Stunned and feeling he was out of his mind,

Elias wondered what that kind of life would mean. He began to wonder what the other beings of the forest were like. Slurring his words, Elias asked her questions.

"Other girls and boys of the forest? Don't they grow up? What do you mean?"

Lia said nothing but sang a mysterious and alluring chant in an unfamiliar language that snared his complete attention.

"Do I have to decide to, ah…do I have to make up my mind now?"

The sweet vapors intensified. She said nothing. With graceful movement, she plunged deep below the surface of the water. Without warning she emerged before him, causing little disturbance in the water. Her face appeared only inches from his and her eyes looked into his. Her alluring eyes and perfect features charmed Elias. She reached for the amulet. Keeping her eyes on his, she held the amulet in her open palm.

"Oh Elias, you most definitely won't need this silly thing anymore. Give it to me so you may join us?"

At that moment, the Turul swooped down within inches of her head, letting out a shrieking caw.

Startled, she looked up to see what the

commotion was. With a jolt, which seemed to come from nowhere, Elias realized she was cunningly drawing his will from his body. He knew that the only way he could free himself from her curse was to find that place of reason in his own core and resist the temptations she was dangling in front of him. As the haze of his mind began to lift, he knew that what she said was too good to be true and this would be giving up on himself. *This isn't right. Talking about sucking out your soul,* he thought.

He grabbed her wrist, which was still holding the amulet, and with a clear mind he said, "Something inside of me—and I don't know what—is reminding me of who I am, and I cannot let you, a Sarkany or anyone else take from me what is mine."

With all of the strength he could find, Elias pushed her away. He turned his back to her and waded to the shore. Exhausted, but returning to his normal self, he sat next to Cimbora, who was just coming out of the spell.

Elias heard a rustle in the tall grass but it grew fainter by the second. The swish of the sound became more of a whisper as it gradually evaporated deep into the dark and enchanted woods.

FIFTEEN

Secret of Fire

E lias' journey, thus far, was unlike anything he could ever imagine. Like a puzzle only beginning to take shape, he now began to appreciate what came from the threats of each twist of danger he faced. Elias marveled at how each menace he encountered wore a cloak of fantasy but, at the same time, was stone cold real.

Elias now realized that his perils could appear sweet or ghoulish and what was beautiful could be venomous. What seemed familiar could deceive. Hideous now presented a new meaning. Each irregular piece of the picture floated freely in his head but they just didn't all connect—not yet. He frowned, unsure of how they would all come together.

He began to think about Nattymama and his thoughts gave way to feelings about the others back home. Elias missed his family. Swallowing the lump in his throat, he wondered what they must have thought when he left without saying good-bye.

Yanking his thoughts away from that subject, he realized he should never have questioned Nattymama. He chuckled to himself thinking of his recent encounter in the woods. He trusted her wisdom and realized that, only by doing so, he would find his answers. This would be the only way his personal mystery would make sense…but *when*?

Certainly, Nattymama must have explained to his family why he left the way he did. That didn't matter so much but the warm embrace of Mama and, albeit infrequent smile of approval from Papa, was on the forefront of his mind. He could not bring himself to hate his father no matter what. Papa was not his enemy.

Wrestling with his brothers and looking after his sisters were activities he thought he would never miss…but he was wrong. He was homesick. Before allowing his mind to slip too far in that direction, he forced himself to turn his mind back to his quest. This was his personal search and his alone. Each step would obviously lead him through an intimate and vital experience that would open his eyes to see life in new and wondrous ways. He knew he could be indecisive and that he lacked confidence most times. He knew he gave others too much say about matters of the heart—his heart. The time was ripe for a new way if he was going to be true to himself.

As Elias and Cimbora hiked over a meandering trail in a forgotten patch of land, Elias caught a whiff of smoke. Continuing onward, he saw puffs of smoke billowing above the treetops from a chimney or campfire. With only one swallow left in his canteen, he was thirsty and tired. Perhaps the smoke would lead him to a kind soul who would allow him to fill his canteen and rest a while.

He came to an old stone bungalow with its large chimney that supplied the ashen fumes pouring into the sky. All was calm and quiet and as he cautiously edged closer to the house, he observed that the front door was slightly ajar. He knocked on the heavy wooden door. Waiting for what he felt was a long time, he tilted his head carefully and peered, unobtrusively, into the house. His angle was poor, and he saw no one.

Elias thought it odd that such a ferocious fire and heavy smoke would puff from the chimney if no one were tending to it in the house. He knocked again, louder this time, but still no answer. Cimbora barked and, with his head straight as an arrow, he plowed through the partially opened door and went directly to another interior opening. He howled, and looking back at Elias, waited anxiously for him. Elias nervously entered the house. Unsure what he would find, he joined Cimbora. With a forceful jerk, he pulled open the door. There sat a man who someone gagged and bound to a chair. Elias rushed in and pulled the dirty rag from his mouth.

"Oh, thank you, my good boy, thank you," the man blurted out with a slight lisp.

"What happened here?"

"I was robbed again. Well, they didn't get anything, *again*, so they tied me up, *again*, and left me here, *again*. I've been sitting here for the better part of an hour," he said.

"Robbed! Again?"

"Yes, it comes with the profession, I suppose."

"The profession? What do you do?"

"I'm a goldsmith. I make jewelry and crowns for the nobility—things like that. Please untie me and then we can talk all you want. This rope is beginning to cut off the circulation in my hands, and I can't have that. They are much too valuable."

"Oh, of course." Elias untied the ropes and freed the man who, at once began wiggling his fingers. He sighed with pleasure.

"That's better," the man said as he massaged each wrist. "Will you join me for some tea?" Unfazed by the ordeal, the goldsmith stood, brushed himself off. He walked out of the room into the larger front room. Elias and Cimbora followed.

"Can I have some water, please?"

The goldsmith retrieved a cup and filled it with water from a pitcher already on the table. He gestured for Elias to sit down and the goldsmith put a teapot on the stove and began to tidy up his home.

"I don't understand," said Elias. "Thieves broke down your door, and tried to rob you. They tied you up, leaving you to die, and you're okay with that? By the way, my name is Elias."

"You are so right! That is, with the exception of dying, Elias," clearly enunciating his name. "I always manage to get freed somehow. Oh, thank you for helping me this time. My name is Gaspar," he said, emphasizing the last syllable of his name.

Gaspar was tall and thin with blonde hair that he carefully parted in the center of his elongated and angular face. His beak-like nose matched his hands and fingers, as they were long and wiry. He wore black. His home was plain and sparsely decorated, but his bench for his craft was ornate and contained a variety of hammers, pliers, and torches. To one end was a pristine, perfectly balanced scale. He had shelves of crucibles, drawers of burs and boxes of chemicals. There were magnifying glasses and files rounding out his work area.

He stopped what he was doing and looked directly at Elias to size him up. Gaspar rolled his eyes and, as if he was exasperated, he said, "I guess I owe you more than uttering the words thank you." He pirouetted and glided across the floor. He fell back into an oversized upholstered chair, and crossed his legs. "Gigantic risks but monstrous rewards," he said.

"Huh?"

Gaspar leaned toward Elias and said dramatically, "This ancient craft I practice is one of harrowing risks but the material benefits make me a disgustingly wealthy man."

Elias could not help but notice that Gaspar's humble and spartanly afforded home seemed anything but that of a wealthy man, especially one who was enthralled with gold.

"Gaspar, what do you do with your riches? I mean, if you have a vast fortune."

"Ah, good question. My treasure is locked away for me, myself and I," he laughed. "Otherwise, I WOULD be robbed."

"I see, but if you can't enjoy it then…"

Not interested in waiting for Elias to complete his thought, Gaspar retorted, "My dexterity is second to none, and my vision is better than an eagle's eye. My papa knew this about me and sent me to become the apprentice of the greatest goldsmith in Hungary— Ambrus. Ambrus taught me how to estimate worth, to determine the purity of gold, and to appreciate the secret of fire.

That is the key, my young Elias, fire! How hot and how long. I can make anything out of gold with a beauty that is exquisite. Did I say exquisite? I *mean* exquisite," he said spelling out the word and then went on to say, "It fetches me a filthy fortune. I *know* the secret of fire."

"Gaspar, you're not making any sense. You have a talent and skill and make a fortune from that but you keep it locked away because robbers are lurking close by. Many wealthy people live like…well, wealthy people. Why do you choose to live like this? Do you share your wealth with a special someone?" Elias said.

Gaspar grew agitated as Elias spoke but shifted quickly to lightheartedness and said, "It's mine, and I will do with it what I please. No, I don't want to share it with anyone. Why would I do a thing like that? Once you share your wealth, it is all over. I'd rather live alone."

His tone became more serious and he continued, "Look at you. You are nothing but a vagabond. You are probably wondering where I keep my treasure just hoping to get your grubby little hands on it. Just like those common thieves, you will never find it. Go ahead. Search for it all you wish. Oh, my robber friends think they will find it if they keep me alive. I am no good to them dead. The secret is in my head."

"Just like the secret of fire?" Elias interjected.

"Precisely. My secrets give me power. Wealth and power—it has a nice ring."

"You have nothing to worry about. I am not a thief, and I don't want *your* treasure or any of *your* secrets. Not if it means I will become cynical and lonely."

Inspecting his hands and pretending to pay no attention to what Elias was saying, Gaspar said, "I believe you. There's something about you. You are not a thief. But my advice to you is this: life is about risk and reward. The greater the risk, the greater the reward. Once you have your prize you must know what to do with it. I choose to lock mine up and take it out only when I see fit. You can choose to do whatever you want with yours ... do you follow?"

"Yes, I hear you," he said in disbelief.

"That is, if you ever achieve anything. But, Elias, as I spend my time assessing life and placing value on what is most important to us mortals, I would say you might never reap any significant reward. I could be wrong but that is a rarity. Well, at least the kind of reward that buys you things."

Elias shook his head in disgust but kept his

thoughts to himself. As he downed the water, his head tilted back, Gaspar observed his every move intently and noticed what he was wearing around his neck.

"Thanks for the water. We'll be leaving now."

With a pleasant lilt to his voice, Gaspar said, "Elias, wait. You haven't finished."

"Oh, I'm all done here."

"Perhaps I was a bit too harsh. After all, I was young and impetuous at one time. Please fill your canteen. Don't rush off. By the way, what is that dangling from your neck?"

Elias pulled the amulet out from under his shirt. When he did, Gaspar's eyes beamed. "That is magnificent ... exquisite! He held out his hand for it. "May I inspect it more closely? You may trust me, I know about such things. I can tell just by looking at it from here that the piece is a masterpiece. I am aware of how valuable it is."

Elias laughed. "After what you just told me, do you really expect me to hand you this amulet? I may not want your treasure, but now, perhaps, you want mine."

Erupting into anger, Gaspar exclaimed, "You are a disgusting young man and I want you out of my house."

Just as fast as he had become inflamed, Gaspar settled himself as he fanned his face.

"I am happy to leave as this hour has been about nothing but you and your fortune. You keep it locked away and don't even enjoy it. For someone who lives for the material world, you don't even take pleasure in it or help others with your work. The beauty of what you do is lost. LOST! Watch out, because next time the thieves may decide you are no longer worth their wait. Sir, I am happy to leave, and I know that what I own will never get the best of me."

"My obnoxious young friend, I am not as deranged as you would paint me. My advice to you is not to let what you *don't* have get the best of you. I am not an evil man, and believe me, I wish you well."

Still distrustful of Gaspar, Elias calmed his nerves and felt no ill feeling for the man. He headed for the door, intent on leaving.

"The heat tells you how close and how long. When you think about it, it has been *too* long," said Gaspar in a low monotone.

Elias turned to look at him and asked, "What

are you talking about?"

"When something is precious, you must know how close and how long to expose it to what could destroy *it*. You feel *it*. You don't *think it*. Fire is an agent of change—both for good and bad. That, my young friend, is the secret of fire."

Elias shook his head and smiled. "This makes no sense. Why are you telling me this *secret?*"

"Seeing that amulet draped around your neck permits me such freedoms. I know you are on a personal quest and although I don't share my worldly wealth, I am forthcoming with what I have here." Gaspar raised his hand and pointed his index finger to his heart.

Perplexed at the sudden shift in their relationship, Elias merely nodded.

"Gold, you see," Gaspar said, "is the most valuable material known to man. Its enduring beauty captivates most, but unlike other metals, it never rusts and is resilient beyond compare. No other substance is anywhere near as versatile. Nothing transforms or changes it. You may strengthen it, but never weaken it. There is an agent dissolves it, as everything has flaws.

However, that takes some doing. That I won't get into. But, my good boy, I digress … do you know why it is most valued?"

Elias shrugged and shook his head.

"It cannot be created nor destroyed. Many have tried, but I have never been interested in either. Do you know what I'm talking about?"

"Of course, you are telling me about gold. That's what you said."

"No, my boy. I'm talking about your heart."

"You're confusing me."

"I have to disagree with you, Elias. I think what I have told you is simple. Man makes such things confusing. But I am only interested in this: gold is nothing but the symbol of the human heart, and that is what makes it more valuable than any other substance known to man. It transforms. *You* decide if I am talking about gold, your heart or, perhaps, both.

"You are a very complex man, Gaspar, and I misjudged you. I'm sorry for having done that."

"No, Elias, you did not misjudge me. I am complex and seldom understood, but thank you for your admission. This is an important step to finding your own value and the secrets we keep inside."

"I think I should be on my way," Elias said.

"Yes, Elias, it's time for you to go and I, for one, have gotten myself out of many a pickle. That being a fact, I have one more word of caution for you. You will see three paths as you leave this house. Do not take the one in the middle. Never take the one in the middle. Take the one to the east, as so many have taken the others. I see them backtrack and never fulfill their journey."

Still not totally sold on Gaspar's change of heart, Elias said, "Thanks, but if you don't mind, I have a friend in the sky who gives me directions."

Unsure whether to trust Gaspar at this point, Elias began to walk. Cimbora raced ahead and sniffed the entrance to one of the paths. Elias looked above for his compass, and the Turul was freely gliding in figure eights above the path headed east. Elias turned to Gaspar and said, "Looks like I'm taking the path to the east."

Gaspar turned and closed the door and said to himself, "The boy has a heart of gold."

SIXTEEN

Third Fear

As Elias ventured deeper into the dark woods, he thought of his time with Gaspar. *What a strange man he is,* Elias thought. *All that gold and he has nothing to show for it. Is his secret really a secret? Does it have meaning? Isn't it obvious?* As he thought more about him, he decided that in all of his bluster and drama, he was genuine. *It is sometimes very difficult to determine what is real and what is not,* he thought, *especially throughout this journey.*

With dusk approaching, Elias searched to find a suitable place to camp. Seeing little other than shadows cast by magnificent trees, he knew he better pick up his pace before the shadows blended into one. He needed to build a fire. Night was riding in with the speed of a stallion leaving the day behind as an afterthought. Having decided on just the right spot, he pulled off his knapsack with his sword still securely tied in place and dropped it beneath one of the massive tree trunks.

With little sunlight remaining, a strange chill in

the air whipped in and out of his camp, so he scurried to gather kindling for a fire. With flint he pulled from a small pocket in his knapsack, he tried to ignite the fuel he had gathered for his warmth and comfort for the unusually cool night ahead.

Having trouble starting any kind of flame with his flint, he thought of Gaspar's secret and laughed to himself. Soon a spark turned into a flicker and then a fledgling flame. Elias nurtured it into a steady fire. He sat close to the heat as it radiated from the glow of the flames. Once he had settled down, he now paid attention to the hunger he previously ignored. Reaching for his knapsack, he found some stale bread, a few hard carrots, and slivers of dried meat. He and Cimbora feasted by the light and crackle of the blaze.

Not yet ready for sleep and somewhat at a loose end, Elias pulled his sword from the knot on his pack. He studied it carefully and examined every angle, mark and design. He had never inspected it closely before, and was surprised to discover an inscription engraved near the hilt. He squinted to make out the letters, but that didn't help. He then leaned closer to the raging fire and held the sword close to the flames for more light.

He felt the intensity of the heat as it nearly singed the hair on his arm. Risking a burn, he held it long enough to finally determine what was etched in the blade. He mouthed the words, *exsisto verus ut vestri*. Backing away from the fire, he wondered for a moment what it could possibly mean.

Elias gently rubbed his arm and put the sword back at his side and tucking away his thoughts with it. He huddled next to the fire with Cimbora curled up against him. As the fire went from a roar to an intense glow, it gave off sufficient heat from its vivid orange and red embers. Elias folded his arms and stared into the flames and hot glimmering coals. Thinking about the inscription and not having a clue what it could mean, he cleared his mind. Suddenly exhausted, he closed his eyes and fell into a deep sleep.

*****

The first rays of the sun grazed the violet and amber outline of the morning clouds and warmly filtered through the enormous boughs of the trees. The leaves were at rest and the air was completely still. Even the birds were hushed as Elias came out of a troubled dream and forcing himself awake. Moving his head back and forth while letting out incoherent mumbles, he lay on the ground with his eyes tightly closed but now he was half-awake.

It was at that moment he felt a sharp point, like the tip of his sickle, pressing squarely in the middle of his chest. To his horror, as he opened his eyes, the point was the tip of his own sword. It was just barely resting on his skin through an opening of the design of his amulet. A sudden move would be all that it would take, and he would suffer a wound from the lifeless steel that had once protected him.

The perpetrator knew Elias' fear paralyzed him and that he would not react. The intruder then slowly retracted the tip of the blade from his chest. He stood over him. Elias tried to make sense of the situation and looked up at the trespasser, but he could see nothing but his silhouette against a fiery backdrop. Elias looked to one side and saw Cimbora muzzled and tied to a tree. He could hear the pounding of his own heart thumping in his ears. His throat tightened.

As the intruder moved slightly to one side, Elias focused on his face. He couldn't believe his eyes—what he saw left him shaken. Perhaps his brain was deceiving him and what he saw was a hallucination. The more Elias focused, he realized who stood above him. It was none other than he, himself, staring down with an unfamiliar and sickening grin. He now knew he was peering at the third and final head of the Sarkany…that happened to be his own.

"If you must, do it now and make it quick," Elias shouted.

"You've read too many stories, and besides, who are you to give me an order?" his captor laughed. "I wish it were that easy. If only it *were* as simple as that," the Sarkany continued with delight.

"What do you mean?"

"Later. Now sit up!" it shouted. The Sarkany backed away with the sword but elevated the gleaming blade backing up about ten paces. The Sarkany then sat on a large boulder next to where he had tied Cimbora to a tree. Elias cautiously sat up and knew he was in a shaky spot.

"As you can see, the dog's okay but I gobbled up the bird for dinner last night," Elias' impostor said with a gruesome smirk.

Upset with hearing of the horrible loss of his

friend, the Turul, Elias could not absorb all he was hearing. Taking a deep breath, Elias gathered his courage and wore it like armor; his eyes never left the Sarkany for a moment. As he focused, Elias went from being repulsed to bewildered. *Is that what I look like? Is that how I move? Certainly, that's not how I am*, he thought.

"You are bothered by this turn of events, aren't you?"

"Yeah, I would say so," Elias said with sarcasm.

"Maybe I should paint you a picture. I first came to you as your hollow self. Like an empty vessel, others try to fill you up with what is important to them. That was Viktor. You will become that hideous soul if you do not find your way—and it does not appear you will. But somehow, you escaped that fate."

"You're pathetic. You don't know what you're talking about," Elias said.

"Oh really? I then came to you as doubt and guilt, as none other than Nattymama. I almost had you. It was that stupid amulet. I had no idea it was hers."

"Yeah, I knew it was you all along."

"But today, I come to you as something that is buried deep in your soul."

"Deep in my soul?" Elias asked in disbelief.

"Today, I come to you as none other than your greatest fear. I am *you* with no pretense and no disguise. I come, once and for all, to take that amulet from your neck."

"You could have done so by force as I slept with my own sword at my heart. You could have easily killed me and taken the amulet," said Elias.

"Yes, you are right, but I did not come to kill you. See, Sarkanys do not kill. We allow our victim to destroy himself. Most of humankind does not need help from anyone or anything to destroy who they are. They summon enough negative force from within to implode. Today, however, all I want is that stupid amulet. You may make it easy and surrender it to me, or I will take it by force. At least that way I will allow you to fight for something."

"You may look like me, but I am not as dim-witted as you. You've already shown your hand when you said you will not kill me."

"Now, now, Elias. Calling me dim-witted will not get you to where you want to go. I did say I would not kill you, but I didn't say I wouldn't maim you, now did I? Anyway, you have already lost your way. When was the last time you pulled out your sketchbook and pencil? Huh? *That* doesn't seem to mean much to you anymore. It seems this sword has captivated you. Perhaps you are more suited being a soldier?"

Elias thought for a moment and reached for his satchel.

"Oh, you won't find it there. Your sketchbook is lost in the forest and you haven't given it a moment's thought. Can't be that important."

Elias was startled, especially as he realized that the Sarkany was correct. It was true that he had lost it, and its whereabouts had not entered his mind until this very moment. A sense of self-betrayal overcame him.

"Elias, you are on a downward spiral. You've been through so much and you're unsure of where you are going. You are doing what so many humans do. You've started out with good intentions. It is over! You will live like so many others, in mediocrity. So hand it over!"

In a quandary, Elias was fearful of what the Sarkany was capable of doing. He didn't know what could or would emerge. He thought of the strange beings of the woods and wondered if he, somehow, was on the way to becoming one of them—an inhabitant of the Under World. Controlled and without a soul, Elias knew the Sarkany had nothing to lose. It was at that moment that he knew he had too much at stake to do nothing. *I can't let this shell of me defeat me.* Impulsively, he stood up.

"What do you think you are doing?" asked the Sarkany.

"I must fight you."

The Sarkany laughed at Elias. "You are relentless. Your only hope is to snatch this sword from my hand and, by the way, I am equally as skilled with my right as my left. After all, Elias, I am an exact copy of you. Now, do you really think you can pry this blade from my hand? Look at you!"

As Elias began to advance. With a stiff arm, the Sarkany pointed the sword at Cimbora, halting Elias in his tracks.

"I said I would not kill you, but I didn't say anything about the dog. Come closer and you can say good-bye to your companion. Lovely name you gave him. 'My companion.' How quaint."

"Shut up! You ARE a coward."

"All I want is the amulet. Easy as that!"

"What's so special about it? Why do you want it so badly?"

"Without it, you are nothing. It actually does nothing for me. I am, and will forever be, the fear in every person that walks this earth."

Elias was frightened and confused beyond reason. He looked at his friend and, in his heart, did not want to take a chance with another's life. Feeling like he had no choice in the matter, he reached for the amulet and yanked it from his neck. He looked at it as it rested in the palm of his hand, and he held it out to the Sarkany. He seemed to be freely giving it to his archenemy. With little warning, he drew back his hand and gently tossed the amulet onto the hot coals.

"There you go."

Guarded, the Sarkany took a few steps toward Elias and paused. No one said anything. Elias stepped toward the Sarkany until they stood inches apart. Elias felt its hot breath and as they peered ever so briefly into each other's eyes. Elias saw emptiness.

"You'll have no trouble fishing it out from the

coals. Where you come from, you're used to it," Elias said breaking the silence.

With that, the Sarkany raised the sword to Elias and with unbelievable force crashed the hilt to the side of his head. He fell unconscious at the base of the tree.

SEVENTEEN

Zoltan

Elias awoke but kept his eyes shut. All he heard was the sound of water dripping. *Drip, drip, drip.* Dazed, he lay motionless. His bandaged head was throbbing. Slowly he opened his eyes and tried to focus. He was confused because someone had tended to his wound but had bound his wrists and ankles. Using every muscle in his arms, he wiggled and pulled the ropes the best he could in order to free himself. It was no use. Haggard and weak, he had no choice but to remain still.

Soft, cool wafts of air filtered in and out of the gigantic room. Only lightened by a small fire and torches mounted to the uneven walls, the room was strange but lent him a sense of ease.

Drip, drip, drip. There were no doorways, only what appeared to be dark passageways at several points along the shiny stone walls. As best as he could tell, they were crooked, winding and misleading.

His vision was now restored, and he focused his

eyes and saw stalactites above him—*drip, drip, drip*. They were gold, pink, various shades of reds, and browns; no two figures the same. The flames flickered, casting ghostly images all around him. *How did I get here? Who tied me up? Who bandaged my head? Where am I?* Questions filled his aching head. Exhausted and bewildered, he lay limp, trying not to move a muscle.

No more than an hour passed before he heard the slow, rhythmic cadence of footsteps growing louder. He closed his eyes and kept each eyelid tight against the other. He was defenseless and felt like an unsuspecting carp nearing the surface of a lake as an osprey readied to plunge toward it from overhead.

As the sounds of the stranger's footsteps grew louder and with each leather sole that hit the rocky surface, he felt his body tense up. His heart raced and was just about to leap from his chest when the sound ceased. The footsteps stopped. After what seemed to be an eternity, Elias pried open his eyes and before him, he saw a thin older man with a rather long white beard. The man peered down at him through half glasses.

"Are you Ordak?" Elias blurted out, fearing his own demise.

"Ordak? To the contrary, my dear boy," said the man with a faint laugh.

Elias studied the man's features, and he realized who stood over him.

"You are…you are the man at the square that day. Yeah, that's who you are. The man who actually liked my paintings."

"Yes, Elias, I am one and the same."

"How do you know my name?" Elias asked.

"You signed my painting," he said as he paused for a moment maintaining eye contact with him. "Elias, I've been expecting you."

"Expecting me? Who are you?

The man cast a soft and tender grin. Like a bolt of lightning, Elias knew.

"Could you be…? You must be Zoltan!"

"Yes, I am known by that name."

Cimbora, who was sleeping at Elias' foot, awoke at the introduction, walked to Zoltan and sat at his feet.

"Good boy, Okos, you are a good friend indeed."

"What? His name is Cimbora, and he's my

dog," Elias said, irritated by this stranger's apparent personal knowledge of his dog.

"No, his name is Okos, and he is as clever as he can be. He is a free spirit and belongs to all of us. But he lives here. He was with me, and you for that matter, on that day we met. I trust you named him Cimbora because he has been a faithful companion."

"He's a good dog," said Elias as he looked at Cimbora and smiled.

Zoltan knelt down to pet the dog.

"Tell me, Elias, about this knot on your head."

"Last thing I remember, I was captured by a Sarkany that… that looked like me. I thought the whole idea of these creatures was to disguise themselves and trick their victim. Seeing me was anything other than a disguise. The moment I saw 'me' I knew it was him. Anyway, it was the weirdest thing."

"Well, don't let that fool you, Elias. You have witnessed the worst kind of Sarkany. You may count yourself fortunate to escape with only a bump on the head. I fought one when I was about your age and lost a finger."

Zoltan showed him his right hand. Elias

grimaced and was mystified.

"I see five fingers," said Elias.

"The difference is that I was born with six fingers on my right hand. Yes, I am a Taltos or some call me a sorcerer—either will do."

"Why six fingers?"

"It is to remind us, each and every day, of our difference and our unique burden and obligation. I am on the side of the good guys, so to speak. However, *my* story is unimportant. Elias, you must tell me more."

"I will. But why did you tie me up? Can you please untie me?"

Zoltan began to loosen the rope and continued, "Clearly I did not want you to move. Some of the Bubus merely tied your hands and ankles so you would not leave before we had the chance to meet. We need some time together."

"The what?"

"Bubus. They are my small friends who live with me. They don't venture far from the cave. They carried you here and saved you from further danger. I assure you, they are quite friendly. Aren't you?" Zoltan looked around the room and nodded his head.

"What? I don't see them."

"That is because you do not know what you are looking for. They are as plain as the bump on your head."

"Huh?"

"They are tiny and determined creatures who have a knack for blending into the walls of the caves. They say next to nothing but are as loyal as can be." Zoltan looked around the room and asked, "Are you not, my cave spirits?" They didn't respond.

Out of the corner of Elias' eye, he saw part of a wall move like a steamy wave as a Bubus moved closer to where he rested. He could now easily see the creatures.

"Ah, thanks," Elias said.

"Thank you for your help. You may run along and play among the caves with all the others," Zoltan said. With that, the walls seemed to realign and move like vapor forming the shapes of about a dozen Bubus. They ran with amazing speed through one of the passageways.

"But how did I get here?"

"You met the Sarkany at the base of the Tree of

Life. The Tree of Life is only paces from the entrance of this cave. The Turul told me that you were just beyond the entrance."

"The Turul! The Sarkany told me that he ate her for dinner."

Zoltan laughed and asked, "When have you ever known a serpent to tell the truth?"

"But…I didn't know one until recently."

"Unfortunately for you, I miscalculated, and for that, I am sorry. When the Turul told me, I kept her here. I did not want the Sarkany to learn of my whereabouts, as they loathe the Taltos. But I did not think the beast would be so bold as to confront you under the Tree of Life. It shows me that I will learn until I die."

"The Turul told you? She talks?"

"Let's say I know her dialect. There is so much more to living in the cosmos that man just does not understand. But enough about the Turul and my communication skills."

Elias looked at him with skepticism but just shook his head and believed him.

"Never mind these details. This confrontation

you had with a Sarkany, that was your spitting image, gives me grave concerns."

"Grave concerns?" Elias was stunned, and asked. "Why?"

"On your journey, you fought with a beast that had twice your muscle, was fierce beyond compare and you defeated it. You fought one who was masterfully deceitful and quite cunning, and you severed its head with little warning. You did extraordinarily well against them. I have various ways of receiving information, if you will, of your trials and triumphs. Although it is the same beast, it is only THIS incarnation of the Sarkany who is your true nemesis."

"I don't understand at all, Zoltan. If the Sarkany has taken on my likeness, then he is no stronger or smarter than me, right?" Elias asked.

"You have a point, Elias, but don't you see the conundrum in the very point you make?"

Elias stood up, frustrated, and began massaging his sore wrists. Unable to stay still, he paced around the room. His head pounded like a jackhammer with each step. Gently rubbing it, he noticed each step he took was unsure and clumsy. He sat on a stool across from where Zoltan was standing and looked at him with a blank expression on his face.

"No, no, I don't see the problem, Zoltan. I don't see it at all. Please tell me," Elias said with his voice dripping with sarcasm.

"My dear Elias, you have battled yourself and lost. You have come this far and came face to face with your worst enemy, and you gave up."

Elias couldn't believe what he heard. "It was going to kill Cimbora!" he said.

"Was it really? He said he would kill the dog, but again, I have never known a serpent to tell the truth," Zoltan insisted.

"Stop it! Stop it! So how can you tell what's the truth? Anyway, you just said that the Sarkany was me yet you call him a serpent. This is all very confusing."

"Calm down, my boy. I must say what I have heard is true. Artists ARE hotheaded. Please Elias, pull yourself together."

"Okay, I'm calm but didn't you call me a serpent?" Elias asked.

"You jumped the gun. No, I did not call you a serpent. What makes you different from that serpent is your true essence. That is what he does not have, trust me. All mortals have a tendency to let Ordak take over, but Ordak is not our essence. Ordak is the negative vibration in the cosmos and he merely contaminates what's good—that is, if good allows it. The Sarkany has nothing inside it but that negative vibration," Zoltan insisted.

"So are you saying that the Sarkany is made up of dark forces, but I have the power to fight off those forces?" Elias asked.

"Exactly. The beast can never completely enter our hearts. You must persevere through all he throws your way. It may not be easy but we control who we are and who we become. We must ask the question of which way we shall go. Which way, Elias, will *you* go?"

"I don't understand what you're asking me. Of course I don't want to go to the way of dark forces," Elias said.

"Let me put it this way, from the moment you were struck on the head, you will forever be looking over your shoulder. You will always question and doubt yourself. You will forever be looking for what is rightfully yours," Zoltan said.

With fear and reluctance evident in his voice, Elias said, "Then I should find this beast and destroy it like the others."

"Precisely. You must find him before he finds you. You must fight the Sarkany that looks like you and you must conquer this beast."

"I'm ready. I've got to find him," Elias reacted.

"Not so fast. You must remember the one statement he made that *is* true. He does not destroy his victim but allows his victim to destroy himself."

"I remember that," Elias said.

"The Sarkany is cunning, defeating him is the only way you will find your fortune—your answer. If you do not destroy him, you will never find what you are searching for, nor will you ever know what's in your heart. You will never experience your dreams," Zoltan said with a concerned look on his face.

Reluctantly, Elias asked, "Why must this be so difficult? I didn't bargain for this. Nattymama told me that if I got to you, you would guide me to my fortune. Not this!"

"And how is what you just described any different from what I have just told you?" Zoltan asked as a matter of fact.

"Well, I thought you were going to tell me how to find my fortune, not...not..."

With a hearty laugh, Zoltan asked, "Oh, you want these things given to you? You want me or someone else to tell you. My son, life does not work that way. Yes, Nattymama or I can guide you, but you must be willing to find your way. After all, your way is different from mine...or Nattymama's."

Elias shook his head and sat down. His stomach sunk and the pounding in his head started again. "I gave him the amulet."

"I know, Elias. It was the first thing that came to mind when I didn't see it around your neck," Zoltan said.

"But, but..."

"No buts, Elias. I assume you didn't know the meaning of the amulet?"

"No, Zoltan, I didn't. I...thought I did. But no one told me."

"Ah, that illustrates my point. You thought someone was going to tell you how precious the amulet was and what it means?"

"Yes, you could say that," answered Elias.

"Elias, could you not see the omens along the way? Could you not see its value? Were there not beings, of all shapes and sizes, who expressed their desire and desperation to seize the amulet? Were there some who learned of it and merely bid you well?"

"Uh…yes, there were more than I want to remember."

"My dear boy, anything worth living for is worth dying for. If we never felt threatened, we would never need to be courageous. If we never felt sadness, we wouldn't know what joy felt like. If we do not know darkness, we may never appreciate our light—your light, Elias."

"You're right. I mean, if you put it that way. I… I screwed up."

"No sulking. You merely took another path. All is not lost. There are more paths—plenty more. It is time to journey on, yet, on another trail. It is the way. It is the natural order of things. It is about being who you are and it takes some doing to pull it all together."

"Then I must leave at dawn and search for the Sarkany," Elias said leaping from where he sat.

Zoltan erupted in laughter and asked, "Where will you find the beast? What will you do when you confront him? He has your sword...and the amulet."

"Hmm, I know where you're going with this," smirked Elias.

"If you are fortunate enough to destroy the beast, are you ready for the consequences, whatever they might be?"

"Well, yes." Elias said with hesitation.

"Your impetuous spirit is refreshing for this old sorcerer, but youth must learn from age or it will be forever arrogant. At dawn, you will travel with me to Budapest. You still have much to experience, witness, and learn before you set out to find the beast."

EIGHTEEN

Hope

At dawn, Zoltan woke Elias from a deep sleep. He gave him a mug of black coffee and a hardboiled egg, but not much time to eat. Zoltan urged him to eat fast and to follow him out of the cave. Stubborn and sleepy, Elias took his time. Bothered at his slow response, Zoltan said nothing, turned, and walked away from where Elias sat. Gulping the coffee, he hurried to catch up with the old Taltos.

"That a boy! Now you're moving. I forgot how teenagers are slow going in the morning. But we must be on our way. We have a two-kilometer jaunt to the river where we catch the ferry. Quickly, quickly, we haven't time to waste."

They boarded the ferry and took their seats away from the few passengers already aboard. It only dawned on Elias as they found their seats that he had never been on a boat.

The ferry shoved off and trolled down the

Danube River. As Zoltan sat peacefully with his eyes closed, Elias was awestruck at the sights of the city, which was growing even more magnificent as they approached her gates.

The sun was radiant and added a gleam on the surface of the water. Moments later, an enormous white cloud intruded and gave the small, choppy waves a dark enchantment. In fits and starts, the wind kicked up, slightly rocking the boat. With every occurrence, it stirred an emotional contrast deep within him.

"I have never seen a place like this," Elias said in wonder.

Zoltan opened his eyes and said, "Yes, Budapest is a magnificent city."

Zoltan stood and walked to the ship's bow and Elias followed. The breeze danced through Zoltan's white hair, and the sunbeams gave a glint to his eyes.

"It is actually two cities in one. Buda, with its rolling hills is on the western bank of this ancient river, and Pest, being much larger, sits on flat terrain on the eastern bank. In some circles, this city is known as the *Paris of the East*. I happen to think Paris is the Budapest of the west."

Zoltan turned to Elias and winked and they both chuckled.

"I had no idea that the city's borders were so far to the horizon. So many beautiful buildings. It makes my village appear so puny. This place is huge—it's unbelievable!"

"It is more than merely a beautiful and charming city, it is a magical and mystical one."

"Magical?" asked Elias

"...and mystical," replied Zoltan. He continued, "So much has converged here over two millennia, and so many cultures have yearned to come here. All kinds of people from all walks of life bring their ways and much more to this city."

"So who have settled here over the past two thousand years?" Elias asked.

"Romans, and then the Celts settled Obuda, the oldest section of Buda two thousand years ago. Conquests and battles have repelled a variety of cultures but have ultimately blended them as one. So here, you may find the answer to many questions as the knowledge of many civilizations have come together to make one," Zoltan said.

"So now they come for something else I'm sure. I mean the city has long been settled," said Elias.

"They now come here for their fortunes—like you, Elias." Zoltan paused and looked at him intently. He continued. "Some follow their hearts. Some follow their dreams. Artists and sculptors have become part of this city. There are businesses, museums, and monuments mixed in with castles and ancient buildings that attest to the spirit, soul, and heart of our people."

With all of his senses, Elias absorbed the experience as he clung to Zoltan's every word.

"If you were a city, Elias, you would be this quiet gem, with your rare distinctions blending as one. You did not get here by some accident."

Everything was rushing toward Elias all at once like an avalanche. It was almost too much at one time, as the wealth of sights, colors, and smells entered every pore of his body. The bright sun illuminated every corner of every bell tower and domed roof in sight. The blend of the centuries was stunning beyond compare.

Approaching the pier, they disembarked from the ferry and walked a short distance to Vorosmarty Square, named for one of Hungary's renowned poets.

Teeming with people, this was the busiest place in downtown Budapest. Zoltan pointed out various shops, restaurants, and street vendors to his young companion.

To one side artists were painting or sketching the city streets or tall buildings with the Danube and mountains as a backdrop. During their trek, Zoltan pointed out a grand opera hall. Those in Eastern Europe knew this city for its recitals, galas, and national exhibits. They saw people at the height of affluence and those on the edge of mere existence.

"Look ahead, my dear boy," said Zoltan. "We have arrived. Directly in front of us stands Szent Istvan Bazilika. It is only a few inches taller than the Parliament Building in Pest. It rises to three hundred fifteen feet, as does Parliament, and together they symbolize that spiritual thought and worldly thinking are equals."

"Oh really?"

"Well, perhaps spiritual thinking edges worldly thinking by an inch or two," Zoltan added with resounding confidence. "Let's take a look inside, shall we?"

Before them were huge bronze doors that

Artisans from more than a century before had ornamented with depictions of important events. Above the magnificent entrance was the bust of Saint Stephen. To the far sides were enormous bell towers crowned with neo-classical cupolas beautifully ensconced with gold.

Like the blossom of a lily, the gigantic doors to the portal quietly opened, and a cool waft of air laced with sweet incense flowed forth. The pure sounds of the organ underscored the young, angelic voices as they rehearsed.

"Should we go in?" Elias asked hesitantly.

"Of course! We are always welcome."

With great solemnity and reverence, the two entered, passed through the vestibule, and stood in the center aisle. The main sanctuary ahead of them was almost undistinguishable because it was so far away. Still reeling from the sights that had led up to the Basilica that morning, Elias was amazed at all he had witnessed.

Halfway to the sanctuary, Zoltan paused and, without so much as a word, pointed to the far wall. Elias followed Zoltan's slender finger with his eyes.

"We must take a detour," Zoltan said and then led Elias to the outer wall of the great church. "Do you see these paintings?"

"Wow. This huge wall is covered."

"All of these portrayals arose from the talents of Hungarian artists who few know their names, but their artwork touches so many souls. This collection of art reinforces the notion that we are capable of rising to the occasion and achieving something far greater and more significant than our humble selves."

In silence, the two savored the beauty of the paintings. They slowly took in all they could; one by one, as they absorbed every nuance or bold stroke made by each artist.

"Let us continue to the sanctuary," Zoltan said.

They proceeded back to the center aisle. Once there, Zoltan walked to a particular spot and froze. He gracefully tilted his head and neck back to look to the grand ceiling of the center dome. Elias did the same.

"This is awesome. How did they build this place?" Elias asked.

"If I forget, please remind me to tell you something about this dome. But first you must see the relic of Szent Istvan, our first king of Hungary."

"Huh? I don't know what you mean. A relic of a person?"

"It *is* a fascinating story. It is history—the story of humans finding answers. That's all," Zoltan said.

"Right this way, Elias. Just a few steps away is the Holy Right Chapel."

The chapel was in a dimly lit alcove of the enormous cathedral. Here rested the mummified hand of Szent Istvan, the first king and founder of Hungary, who brought Christianity to the nation.

"As gloomy as it may sound to you, this relic symbolizes, to this community, the incorruptible right hand of the divine authority."

"But why are you showing this to me? What does it have to do with me?"

"Szent Istvan died in 1038. Confronted with great peril and immense odds, he followed his heart. He knew what his heart was telling him. He heard a clear voice within him. He knew what he needed to do, and his actions changed Hungary forever!"

"So that's how he became king," Elias said.

"Yes, the people of the time anointed him as

the first king. This, however, is not why I brought you here. I will tell you that in a moment. Follow me."

Elias wondered what this tour was going to tell him about his eventual battle with the Sarkany. He couldn't keep the dragon out of his mind, as he no longer felt the amulet around his neck and close to his heart. He did all he could to keep his mind on what Zoltan was telling him.

"This way, Elias. Follow me," Zoltan said.

At a livelier pace, Zoltan entered a chamber door hidden by marble inlay as Elias picked up his pace and followed. Rushing down dark hallways and through a maze of passageways, Elias could hardly keep up. He knew that if he did not keep an eye on Zoltan, he would be lost. Turning the last corner, Zoltan began to climb a black, rickety staircase. Elias caught up and, out of breath, asked, "Where are we going?"

"Up, of course, my dear Elias. UP!"

"Aside from 'up?'"

"In due time, Elias, in due time."

It became darker as they ascended. Each step Elias took was guesswork, as he had no time to think. At a constant rate, Zoltan seemed to glide. He maintained a steady pace ten steps ahead of Elias. He reached the top and Elias soon joined him, panting and out of breath.

Before them, they saw the threshold of a doorway and, using his shoulder, Zoltan pushed open the heavy wooden door. As it opened, the air was flooded with light. Zoltan walked to the center of the landing. Elias followed him and was thrilled to find that they were directly under the domed roof of the cathedral. This was the highest point in the city.

"Ah, what a wonderful panoramic view of the city," Zoltan exclaimed. "This magnificent structure took fifty-four years to build—fifty-four years, Elias! This Basilica is second only to Saint Peter's in Rome. More than eight thousand people may congregate at any one time directly below this remarkable dome.

Where we stand at this moment, this dome collapsed while under construction, and when it did, many of the artisans and workers lost their lives."

Elias tensed up and nervously peeked over the edge.

"Oh, Elias, not to worry. It is sturdy and is not going anywhere." Zoltan walked to a bench and extended his palm, inviting Elias to join him at his side.

"So what's this have to do with me Zoltan?" Elias said as he stood to look at the horizon.

"See, the heart of humans, Elias, is where all decisions are made," he said as he thumped his chest. "The mummified hand is more than a hand. It represents mere mortals finding, understanding, and embracing who they are. It is about being part of something greater than themselves."

"It's a creepy hand—I don't get it," Elias said.

"See, the hand, Elias, represents the rebirth of hope. For nearly one thousand years, and much to the sorrow of a heavyhearted people, thieves stole the relic for generations at a time. Wicked men sold it and then, they sold it, and so on."

"What a strange thing to sell and buy."

"Some people will do anything for money."

"You're right about that. So what did the people do, and how did it get back here?" asked Elias.

"For many years, due to the actions of these few, the hand remained outside this homeland. During all the trials and tribulations, the heart, spirit, and soul of the people was never broken.

When the people of this city seized it, they brought it here and kept it secure until they could complete the construction of this magnificent place."

Remembering what Zoltan told him a day earlier, Elias said, "So anything worth living for is worth dying for. If we never felt threatened, we would never need to be courageous. If we never felt sadness, we wouldn't know what joy looked like. If we …"

"…do not know darkness, we may never appreciate our light…yes, Elias you have a wonderful memory, and I'm quite honored," said Zoltan.

"Sounds like the people found the power from somewhere inside to keep moving forward," said Elias.

"Yes, people call it all kinds of things, but the collapse of the dome, albeit devastating, was a test. It was evidence of the inspiration we all possess. When we contribute because our heart tells us to, we send vibrations into the cosmos. When we leave this world, our vibration continues. It is our legacy."

"Zoltan, I'm not sure what all of this means to me exactly. I'm not sure how any of this will help me against the Sarkany."

"We may not be the ones to bring a new belief

to a new nation, or possess the ability to create a masterpiece, or be the best wheat farmer in the land. However, we can always be authentic and true to the person we live with every day of our lives—ourselves. When we follow our hearts we are acknowledging our true nature, simple as that. It is *the* gift."

"Sounds good, but it doesn't sound easy."

"True. It's not always easy to recognize what is good or true. But, Elias, when we do not follow our hearts we allow it to be contaminated, and we become vindictive and barren. Others fill our heart as we sit back and allow them to do so. Then we will ask 'what if' or 'if only' for as long as we live. We, then, are destined for a life of gloom."

Elias felt a mix of emotions surge through his body. Not comprehending everything that Zoltan was saying, he sat quietly. Zoltan understood his silence.

"I am merely saying, Elias, that we must know our nature, and only then is it clear that we have no choice in the matter. We are unique in this vast cosmos and we should strive to find our own powers," Zoltan said.

NINETEEN

Tree of Life

Exhausted from their journey to and from Budapest, Elias slept late the next morning. When he rose, the only sign of Zoltan was the breakfast coffee kept warm on hot coals and a hardboiled egg on a small plate. Elias ate in silence. He walked out of the cave into bright sunshine and sat on the ground under The Tree of Life in solitude with his thoughts. He sat at the exact spot he had fallen to his worst fear. Cimbora lay at his feet.

Trying desperately to tie in all his experiences, he brooded and wondered whether or not he was ready to battle the Sarkany.

Zoltan walked up the path from the opposite direction and sat on a stump about twenty paces away. His attention went to a pair of songbirds on a limb of a nearby tree. A minute passed.

"Elias, do you know why I am able to rest my weary bones on this old and decaying stump?"

Elias looked up at him, said nothing but

answered him by shaking his head.

"Fear, Elias, fear. Legend has it that the enormous tree, or the one which is giving you shade right now, produced a sapling that was growing as a healthy tree. A young boy nurtured the tree and would visit it often. It brought him joy to see it grow as it weathered harsh winters and dry summers. That sapling grew for half a century and, as that boy became a man, he returned from time to time. Nevertheless, he would come to sit in solitude to ponder life and reflect on what he found in his soul.

Although the man did not know for sure, he hoped the tree he cared for was an offshoot of the Tree of Life just mere paces away. Over the years as he watched it grow, he would admire them both. His contribution to its growth humbled him.

When the man became old, he came back to spend time and sit under the shade of the tree with a book in hand. As he approached the area, he realized it was too late. A young man with an axe had one or two final swings before the tree fell. To the old man's horror, he saw the tree that once pointed to the heavens fall to the earth.

'What did you do? That was a precious tree and a one of a kind gift to this planet! With all the other trees in this forest, why this one? There must be many trees closer to your home for your fire,' the old man screamed.

The axe man replied, 'Oh, this is not for firewood. I had to destroy this tree because I feared its magnificence would overshadow The Tree of Life. It may have become too beautiful and rival what we have come to know and depend on.'

'You *idiot*!' the old man said. 'You fear the wrong thing. Fear not what may become beautiful and magnificent. There's plenty of room for what is good. Embrace it and become part of it. Destroying what *might be* dishonors today and disregards tomorrow's hope.'

With difficulty, the old man forgave the young man for his wrongdoing. The old man lowered his head, and walked away in great sorrow.

A month later, the old man came back with renewed joy in his heart knowing that the time he had spent sitting under the tree during his long life gave him refuge from a tired and fearful world. He brought with him a sapling that he knew he would never live long enough to see its shade. He planted it and took care of it until he died. It is the tree to my right. It is the tree that brings me delight, and is home of those delightful songbirds."

Elias looked up and saw a beautiful tree.

"Aren't all trees just like The Tree of Life?"

"How so?"

"Well, aren't all trees, or anything for that matter, actually standing at the very center of the world? We live on a round ball," Elias said.

"Precisely. All beings are of value and have their place. I see you have been thinking. Now do you see what I am talking about?"

"Little by little—yeah," said Elias.

"Good, Elias, *good*! Will you tell me what you have learned from your experiences?"

"My deepest fear is not failure by following the path to my dream. My *true* fear is what will become of me if I succeed. If I follow my heart, will others still love me for who I will become? Will I be able to handle success? Will I be honest and kind? Will I become arrogant? Will I still be me?"

"My dear man, let me add that we do a disservice to ourselves and the light of humanity that has come before us, to purposefully be anything other than our authentic self. We cannot strive to be anything less than who we truly are."

"Understanding is one thing—doing it is another," Elias said.

"Yes, Elias you are right. I am embarrassed to say this is why I lost my finger. The finger that made me different and reminded me of who I am. I so desperately wanted to be like the others that I…that I…"

"Say no more," interrupted Elias.

"What I will say is that I regret my actions. I don't want you to regret yours. So, as I see it, you have no choice in the matter."

"I now know the significance of the amulet," said Elias.

"Shush, Elias. Since you know, and I know, we have no need to discuss it, now do we?"

TWENTY

The Answer

Hours later, Zoltan was boiling water and carefully lowered three eggs into the pot. Elias came into the room, looked over Zoltan's shoulder, and shook his head.

"Hard-boiled eggs again? When does it end?" Zoltan continued tending to his chore and paid little attention to Elias' remark. Elias went to the table and sat on a bench.

"How will I know I'm ready to fight the Sarkany?" Elias slumped over the gnarled and knotted table in front of him.

Zoltan remained silent as he poured boiling water from a kettle into two large ceramic mugs. The steam wafted from the cups, and Zoltan inhaled the vapors deeply. He held his breath for several seconds then exhaled. He carefully tended to the tea dunker and placed one mug in front of Elias and one on the opposite side of the table. He unhurriedly pulled out the bench, sat, and looked across to Elias. With hands on either side of the mug and his face slightly over the cup, he again, felt the steam of green tea. Zoltan looked up at Elias, raised one eyebrow and grinned with satisfaction. Elias was not impressed.

"Were you asking me a question?" Zoltan mused.

"You heard me. Why are you acting so weird?"

"Weird? Oh, really, my dear boy."

"Am I ready?"

"That, my boy, is your call."

"You told me I have much to experience, witness, and learn before I leave."

"You are absolutely correct. You are quoting me precisely. I like that."

"Well, then am I ready?"

Zoltan paused and sipped from his hot mug, and the curling steam filtered through his whiskers to his face. Placing the mug on the table, he answered Elias.

"Think, Elias. Are *you* ready? If you must ask, my boy, I would say you are *not* ready." Zoltan leaned toward Elias and looked him squarely in the eyes. "Tell me what questions still hang heavy in your mind? Think!"

Stubborn, Elias shook his head, picked up the cup of piping hot tea and gulped some of the liquid.

"OW! My tongue. I burned my tongue! Why didn't you tell me it was scalding hot?" Elias shouted.

"Yes, I knew you had more questions on your mind." Zoltan raised his shoulders and filled his remark with quiet laughter. "Would you like a boiled egg?"

"Very funny," Elias exclaimed, "and no, I don't want a boiled egg."

"Very well, then."

"As a matter of fact, burning my tongue reminds me of something," Elias said, holding his tongue loosely with his index finger and thumb. "The night before the Sarkany showed up, I took a long look at every detail of my sword. I held it close to my fire and nearly burned myself. It had an inscription."

"Yes, go on, Elias. What did it say?" Zoltan asked, leaning toward him.

"It was in some other language. I think I remember the spelling. It started with 'e'. Let me think."

"Think, boy, think!"

"Oh yeah, it was something like *exsisto verus*, ah, ah…" Elias scratched his head and looked to the ceiling.

"…*ut vestri*," Zoltan whispered. "But of course. It is pronounced *existo verus ut vestri*, and that is Latin for *be true to yourself*."

"That sword is now in the wrong hands, and I must see to it that I get it back from the Sarkany."

Zoltan stood and walked to the far corner of the room, pulling on his earlobe. "So is the amulet, for that matter. Your challenge is mighty. Yes, indeed. But I would say regaining ownership of that sword is not primary. Not at all. It has served you well to this point, but where you end up with the Sarkany, that sword will not help you anymore. That goes for all material objects; they can only take us so far. Now tell me, Elias, during your journey, what else have you learned?"

"Well, Gaspar, the goldsmith, told me a secret."

"Ah, Gaspar. I should have known. What is this secret he spoke of?"

Reaching for a pitcher of water that was on the table, Elias poured some into a cup, took a sip and continued, "He said that fire tells us how close and how long. When you begin to think about it, then it's been too long. I thought what he told me was too obvious to be some sort of secret, but then he told me more."

"Go on, Elias. What else did he say?" Zoltan slowly walked back to the table and sat across from Elias.

"When something is precious, he said, you must know how close and how long to expose it to what could destroy it. You feel it. It's not something to think about but feel."

"Go on, go on," Zoltan pushed Elias.

"Okay, okay. Let me think. Oh yeah, he said that fire changes for good *and* for bad. He was talking about his work with gold."

"Yes…gold, I see. But, Elias, the operative phrase is 'you must know how close and how long to expose it to what could destroy it…feel it…don't think it.' Yes! It is a matter of knowing yourself, your capabilities, and your heart. You have come exceedingly close to the fire, my good boy, and you have done well. As I see it, you have one more such test."

Sighing and wrinkling his nose, Elias sat upright

in his chair. "Let me get this straight. The sword will no longer help me, but I am to confront and fight the Sarkany on *a feeling*?"

Reaching for his mug, Zoltan slurped and said, "Yes. Of course."

"And I must take the amulet from his claws, risking self-destruction?"

Zoltan, again, slurped his drink making more noise than he should before speaking, "Again—yes. I would say that your logic is spot-on."

"He will try to lure me into his trap."

"He has already done so," Zoltan said bluntly while sipping more tea. "You must exercise caution. As for the amulet, you must simply reclaim it."

Standing and walking away from Zoltan, Elias sarcastically asked, "Oh yeah, I'll just walk up to him and ask him if he's done with it…really Zoltan?"

"You have just told yourself how you will reclaim it."

"Huh? I did?"

"Of course, you did. Reverse what you told me."

"I will reclaim the amulet by avoiding a trap."

"You forgot one thing. The sword is in the hands of the Sarkany."

Throwing his hands up, Elias said, "You didn't have to remind me of that."

"Please walk to the trunk on the other side of this room. The one in the corner," Zoltan pointed and continued, "and open it."

Without a question, Elias did what Zoltan told him. Using two hands to raise the heavy lid, he drew back a blanket and at once saw a sword. He grabbed the hilt and pulled it from the ancient trunk.

"Zoltan, it is the twin of the other sword."

"Look again. Read to me what the inscription says."

Elias walked over to the glow of the burning flame of a torch and with some effort he read, "*Exsisto unus per pectus pectoris.* What does that mean?"

"Be one with the heart. Only when the two swords clash shall your true nature shine like the sun. Worlds will open. The other sword served you well until now. This sword will guide you against the Sarkany."

Elias' bemused expression melted into a faint

smile and confident nod.

"Then I am ready to go."

"Your youth brings me great joy. But tell me, are you truly ready?"

"Yes, I am," Elias said looking over his new sword.

Taking another drawn-out gulp from his cup, Zoltan asked, "Where will you go?"

Elias paused, put the sword down and straddled the other end of the bench where Zoltan sat, "Yeah, you have a point. Where do I go?"

"Think. If you were the Sarkany, where would you want to confront *you*?"

"Good question—The Tree of Life? That's where!" Elias blurted.

"Far too risky. He faced you there once before. I suspect he knows you have been with me, and I assume he wants you far from these enchanted woods."

"I know! Nattymama told me that I must return the sword safely when I come home. The Sarkany will be waiting for me there. I know it. Nattymama told me to begin my journey at the Castle of Sirok."

"Absolutely! There lies the inception of your

quest. This is where you stirred your soul and the spirits within. It is your origin. Nattymama knows best. You must always remember where you came from, and it is the only way to find the true path to your future."

"So I go back to go forward?"

"Yes. It is the only way."

"But it has taken me weeks to get here, so I must leave right away," Elias said.

"Elias, it takes many a man much longer to arrive at the point you have now reached. It, however, will take you no time to arrive at a new summit and there you will see measures that are even more amazing. You are sure to find him there, Elias."

"It took me a long time to get here by foot."

"You may take my horse. He is an old and ugly creature, born with six legs but now stands on five, but do not let his outward appearance worry you. My horse has the wisdom of the ages, and he has risen from peril many times, therefore, I call him Star.

You will find him in the meadow thirty-two paces east of the Tree of Life. You will know him at once because he is jet black and has a beautiful mane of silver hair. He, like me, is not much to look at, but he has a heart the size of Budapest, and he flies at the speed of thought. You will be at Sirok by nightfall. Get your sleep and leave at dawn."

"I will. I'm ready…but I'm unsure what I will face when I see the Sarkany."

"Yes, young man, I would say the unknown is frightening, but it is the final battle that detains you from following your heart."

"But how? How do I defeat it?"

"There you go again, asking me questions when you know the answer," said Zoltan.

"This time I don't think I have an answer."

"Remember this, the Sarkany may look like you, but he is not you. He *is not* you. He is dishonest and does not own your experiences. He does not possess your skills and talents or even your characteristics and traits. For instance, you are ambidextrous, are you not?"

"Yes, I can use both hands equally well."

"Remember he does not tell the truth. Unless he, too, is ambidextrous, I would venture a guess and say he is limited. But above everything else, he does not know what is in your heart because he *has* no heart. That is crucial. Do not be put off-guard by his outward appearance. You, Elias, will devise a way to be victorious."

"You're right Zoltan. I will," Elias said with some hesitation.

"Remember, your journey to Sirok is his way of luring you to the fire. Knowing this gives you an advantage."

Elias hung his head and said, "I will find a way."

"Then why are you so sullen?"

"What if I don't...?"

"Stop right there. Remember what Gaspar told you? If you think too much, the flame will burn."

Elias lifted his head and smiled. He looked the old man in the eyes and felt reassured. With his voice shaking a little, Zoltan said, "It all comes down to belief. The cosmos has come together to give you all you need. I believe in you. Nattymama believes in you. Elias, you must believe in yourself. When you believe, we all triumph because you send that vibration into the vastness of the cosmos. Your goodness has a way to affect all."

"I *do* believe in myself."

With that, a tear ran down Zoltan's face, and he

gave Elias a reassuring wink.

"You will not see me again. I bid you well."

"What! What do you mean?"

"Beings come in and out of our lives. In some cases, we are better off for having known them: no matter if it was a moment, a week, or a lifetime. Keep in mind, we must always be certain to reach out and hold on to that part that they so generously gave us. We should emblazon that gift on our own hearts."

"But Zoltan, we have become friends."

"That we have. We should never lock away the gifts we've given each other, but we should share it with others. When we do, we bring great honor to all."

"But there is so much more that I can learn from you," said Elias.

"And I from you. But it is time. The moment is upon us. Your fortune awaits. I must step aside and you must go."

"I am grateful to you. I will never forget you."

Zoltan smiled. "Please understand that when you destroy the Sarkany, you must be ready for the consequences, whatever they might be."

Zoltan paused. He clasped his hands humbly in

front of his waist and reverently bowed his head. As he did, Elias bowed his head in the same manner. Elias stepped up to where Zoltan stood and hugged him. He returned with a tight embrace. The old sorcerer then turned and walked away as a tear rolled down Elias' cheek. Keeping his head down, Elias listened to each step Zoltan took. Eventually, the sound of his footsteps died away until the only thing Elias heard was silence.

TWENTY- ONE

Uncovering Treasure

The five-legged horse was stood faithfully where Zoltan had described. Standing alone in the field, he was feeding on a salt lick. When Elias approached Star, the horse looked up to greet him. Elias tenderly stroked his silver mane and quietly spoke to him.

"I've never seen a horse quite like you, but then again, I've seen so much that no one where I come from would ever believe me for a minute."

Elias continued to run his fingers gently through the strange beast's long, silky mane. Star would occasionally bend his long neck to examine Elias. Looking into his large, chocolate eyes, Elias felt a warm connection with his new companion. He pulled an apple from his pocket and fed it to him.

"We're going to be good friends. I can tell."

Prepared for the quest, Elias noticed a bulging saddlebag on Star. He untied the leather strap. Reaching in without looking, he pulled out a hardboiled egg and his face lit up. Looking in the bag, he saw, among other items, a long wooden box. Attached to the box was a note.

Elias,

Who you are is the birthright given to you by the good forces of the cosmos so fear not. What is, is. Life is the journey and has many turns in its path. Become all it offers.

This box is the holder of something that, if properly used, will ward off evil, as it is the worldly extension of what lies in your heart. Believe. Be true to yourself, and be one with your heart. Although the box is now empty, you will know what once belonged inside and when you least expect it, it will appear. Like this box, it is only when you are empty that you may become full.

Zoltan

Intrigued, Elias opened the box and, and just as the note said, he found nothing.

Feeling more confident, he put the box back into the saddlebag. Suddenly Elias heard barking, and before he knew it, Cimbora had run from the cave to his side. Panting, he sat at Elias' feet. Elias squatted beside his friend and rubbed behind his ears.

Kneeling down, Elias hugged his friend. Trying to be strong, Elias said, "We already said our good-byes a little while ago. I'm sorry, boy, but you've got to stay here. I've got to do this alone. Thanks, my Cimbora. You and I made an awesome pair. I've got to go, boy. I'll come back for you. Promise. Take care of Zoltan."

Elias hugged him one last time, and Cimbora showed his affection by licking Elias' face. Elias heard a familiar caw and beamed. Standing, he looked to the sky. Against the morning hues of pinks and violets, he saw the Turul circling in the lacy clouds. He knew it was time for him to be on his way. With newfound self-confidence, he mounted Star and began a new expedition. He was ready for the journey to Sirok.

*****

As though he was searching for a lost key, Elias retraced his exact steps through the woods. As Star carried him furiously through the forest, Elias thought about the strange beings and creatures he encountered as he maneuvered through this bizarre and bewitched land. Although the Sarkany was the most malevolent and threatening, one by one, each stranger had tried to nurture the seeds of self-loathing, deception, and empty-heartedness that are within us all, he thought.

The other, less detestable beings were perhaps not lethal but nonetheless wretched. Their greed, self-hate, and alluring ways were a way of life for them, as they disregarded what was deep in their own hearts. Hearts created the same way as his.

He knew the creatures had sown poison seeds in his soul. He knew it was up to him, today, to make sure to quash their growth so they could bear no fruit.

Halfway to Sirok, he approached a familiar stone slab that lay near a river. Galloping past it, Elias pulled on the reins and redirected Star to return to the spot.

"I know I need to be here right now. I just know. I feel a force pulling me. This must be Lantos' doing," Elias said to Star as he stroked his long smooth neck.

A few seconds later, he heard the soft, memorable strains of a lute. It was alluring but very different from the song that Lantos knew and played. Elias wondered whom he would find on the other end of the lute.

"It is beautiful just like Lantos' song," he said

squinting his eyes and looking deeper into the forest.

He dismounted Star and walked toward the beautiful music. Clearing brush as he walked and wending his way off the main path he found Lantos with his lute in hand, leaning against a tree. He played the purest of sounds as each note floated from the strings. The lyrics he sang were tender and passionate. Enjoying every moment, Elias sat on the ground waiting for him to finish his performance. He was in absolute admiration of his friend. Lantos strummed his final note and slowly laid his lute down as he looked at Elias.

"That was wonderful, Lantos. But I am shocked. I thought you were content with just one song."

"I thought I was, too. But your light shone on me that day. Let me tell you, I see so many travelers pass my way on their personal journeys just like you. Although many have heard my song, you were the first and only to tell me to learn more. You told me that I have many songs in my soul. When you said that you were running away to find something important, I realized I was running just to run away."

"I knew you had more in you Lantos—I knew it," Elias said.

"You haven't heard the best part," said Lantos.

"The best part? That sounds pretty good to me. What do you mean?" asked Elias.

"After we said our good-byes and you were on your way, I walked to the river, as I do every day, and that's when I came across something. I found something of yours and I knew you would be back."

"I think I know what you must have found," Elias said as if Lantos was going to scold him.

"You forgot something near to your heart."

A sack lay near Lantos on the ground. He turned to rummage through it and pulled out Elias' sketchbook.

"I found this near the river. It appeared to have slipped between two rocks. When I pulled it out, I knew at once it was yours, and one day you would come back for it. I thought you would have come back sooner because this is full of so many wonderful drawings."

"In my search, I hate to say it, I lost my way. When I did, I lost my sketchbook and, I lost sight of it.

229

I'm embarrassed to admit it, but I forgot about it," Elias confessed.

"To me, it is THE symbol of my search," Lantos said. "See, as I happened upon it, I saw hundreds of drawings, not just one. Hundreds! At that moment, I decided not to run away any longer, but run toward something. I taught myself more songs. With each new song I learn, I knew I could still learn more. I don't think it will end. It's something that I feel. So I thank you, Elias."

"You did it, not me. You taught yourself what you already knew and that was inside of you. What are you thanking me for?"

"When I noticed the amulet around your neck, you asked me if I wanted it. You asked me if I knew what it meant," said Lantos.

"Yes, I remember we talked about the amulet."

"Well, I did not want it because it was *your* amulet."

"But others have fought me for *my* amulet and they wanted it even though they knew it was mine," said Elias.

"I understand, but I have come to realize that

we all have an amulet, and it does no good to have another's. We must uncover our own amulet. It is only then that having it makes any difference at all."

"Lantos, I may have showed you that I believed in you, but you needed to decide to believe in yourself."

"Yes, that is true. It was at that moment I had a flash of clarity—of insight. I felt the rhythm of my heart. Perhaps all I needed was a light to show me the way. My life had become easy for me. I hid behind my outward appearance and what others had already decided for me. So, Elias, I found my amulet, and it is buried here," Lantos said, pointing to the center of his immense chest.

*****

It was the end of a glorious day when Elias reached the foot of the mountain. He marveled at the distance he and his miraculous horse covered in one day. Riding since the sun had shone its infant rays, he was amazed as each minute sped forward. More amazing was that each moment was unique and stood alone. His new journey was steady and constant. With his hand shielding the sun from his eyes, he threw his attention to the mountain's peak. There, lay his fate. He imagined that the Sarkany was perched on a sharp boulder and awaiting his arrival.

They began their ascent. The winding path to the summit was all too familiar, but this time his climb was effortless on the back of his mystical steed. As they approached the fork in the path, the five-legged creature intuitively knew the way to go. He knew the pitfalls to avoid, and did so with a blissful grace. The path twisted and was rocky but Star's footing was sure and precise. With each step, Elias sensed his own confidence growing, and he knew there was no turning back. The only way was up.

They arrived at the peak to find the area untouched. They were alone. There were no signs of the Sarkany, and it was eerily still. Shadows lengthened as the evening quickly gave way to the onset of night. The air was becoming cool and strange. Dark clouds with a hint of blood red moved in above, casting shadows on the rocky peaks of Sirok.

He dismounted and looked over the area. As he walked closer to some of the remains of the castle, a gust of wind picked up and stirring the ancient sands of the ruins. Before he could shield his eyes from the onslaught of the pelting debris, the blast of whirling wind died down. He hustled over to the arches where his journey had begun.

"Hello," shouted Elias.

"*Hello, Hello, Hello, He…*," echoed back to him before fading away. With still no sign of the Sarkany, he sat on what was left of a stonewall and peered through the three arches in the same way he had done weeks earlier when he had determined the path that he would not take on his journey.

Randomly, the same stubborn wind kicked up, spinning shards of eroded stones and sand filling the area. Just as the winds became unusually fierce, they oddly settled down.

"He's here Star—he's here."

An hour passed and then another, but still no Sarkany. Star meandered to his side. Looking at the horse, Elias sensed he was telling him to set up camp. It was turning into a cold night and the icy air bit through him. He decided to build a fire. He gathered some brush and used a small hatchet that he found in the saddlebag to chop some small branches from the distorted and fledgling trees. Disfigured vegetation was common in the fortress. He sparked a fire with the kindling he collected, and nurtured the tiny flames by adding more dry brush.

Opening another large pocket on the saddlebag, he found a dagger in its sheath. Surprised but pleased, he pulled it out and examined it closely. With his thumb, he lightly rubbed the blade to determine its sharpness. Pleased with its razor-honed edge, he returned it to the sheath and tied it to his boot. He practiced many times yanking it from its sheath until he felt his movement was natural and precise.

Reaching into the bag again, he pulled out some rations of dried beef and bread along with his canteen. He sat next to the fire, ate his meager supper, and stared into the glow of the fire.

The crackling blaze was hypnotic as his thoughts melted from guarded to pensive. The day had become long, and he was tired. He began to wonder if the Sarkany would make his presence known at Sirok. Thoughts bounced and swirled in his mind, and he began to doubt his own convictions.

His stomach grumbled and he began to feel drowsy. He heard the voices in his head of the old men in the square. He tried to block the images from his mind. He heard Papa's voice as he was discouraging his zeal by giving him the ultimatum. Oddly enough, even the butterfly he saw on his walk to Nattymama's the day he left came into his mind. He thought of how Nattymama set him free although he didn't think that way at the time. He heard Zoltan's voice and in his quiet way, he drowned the others out. He could hear another faint voice deep in his mind. He desperately focused on it but couldn't make sense of it no matter how hard he tried.

The night thickened with cold air so he moved closer to the fire finding all the warmth he could. More hours passed with no sign of the Sarkany, but Elias would not allow himself to sleep. He remembered the harrowing manner in which the beast woke him pointing his own blade at the amulet and nearly piercing his skin. He could not wipe from his mind the sight of the Sarkany as he awoke only to see it straddling him. This was a memory he would rather not relive, but it rebounded in his mind's eye over and over again.

Drained, he saw over the mountaintops the first fingertips of orange sun soften the sky. He couldn't believe it was dawn. To revive himself, he slapped his face and pinched his arm. He gulped from his canteen. Nothing seemed to work. He shouted until his throat hurt, "COWARD." It echoed back at him.

Now enraged, he took his hatchet and heaved it at the wall of the castle. To his surprise, the blade pierced the rock throwing off sparks, but it solidly plowed through the surface and was wedged in the wall.

"Wow."

Now calm, he pulled the hatchet from the wall and chopped some branches from a nearby tree for the fire. He added the sparse fuel to the failing fire and, much to his amazement, the flames doubled in size. It was hotter than it should be which made no sense to him.

With no new timbers, the fire tripled in volume, giving off intense heat.

"Did you really think I would be sitting here waiting for you, Elias?" a voice, *his* voice, came from somewhere nearby. Elias quickly backed away from the fire and found his sword.

"Ha! I see you answered my call. Show yourself, you coward!" Elias exclaimed.

The Sarkany walked around one of the arches. He was rested and clear-eyed. Slowly he walked forward a few paces, sat on the stonewall, and motioned for Elias to remain where he was but to sit down. He was wearing the amulet.

"What a pleasure. You have come to me," he said with a fiendish smile. "Did you come to retrieve *this* old thing?" While looking at Elias, the Sarkany delicately patted the amulet that dangled from his neck.

"Maybe," Elias retorted in a similar, arrogant tone.

"Maybe? Okay, play it that way, but let me tell you something. Every day people look in the mirror and see themselves. Do you know whom they *really* see?

"Don't keep me in suspense. Who?"

"Very funny. They see me. They see their fears. But many put those thoughts aside and go about their business, safe and sound knowing that they had better not disturb the order of things or take any risks in their daily lives."

"I don't fear you," Elias interrupted.

"As I was saying…they don't follow their hearts because they may fail or, better yet, if they succeed, they question whether they can handle the change. Sometimes the chase is all they have in them—the chase, Elias. Is that all you have in you—the chase?"

"You mean nothing to me. I know exactly what you are and I know your ways," Elias said.

"Stop interrupting me. Do you wonder if your family and friends will appreciate you if you do change? Most mortals worry about such things. They agonize whether others will understand them, or even still love them unless they stay the same."

"You're pathetic," Elias mumbled shaking his head.

"In a cruel world, giving up anything that resembles love is quite horrible, wouldn't you agree?"

Elias did not answer. He began to fidget and think of how he could defeat the Sarkany. He acted as if he was paying attention to the beast.

"Despondency is my wicked cousin, and I know him well. Yes, our hearts may set us on an unfamiliar path, but most humans never get to where they want to go. Like you, mortals are afraid of their potential. I say you are not ready to handle what and who you may become, success or failure."

The Sarkany paused and smiled before softening his tone.

"I suggest you be like all the others and follow me. Whether you admit it or not, you have been following me your whole life. I have talked to you in your own head."

He patted the amulet again. Elias was holding back his response and began to think through the details of how he was going to fight for what was his.

"Elias, my righteous half, I am happy to hold on to the amulet a little longer for safekeeping. In fact it would *honor* me to do so."

Elias stood and stepped backward as not to alarm the Sarkany and spoke firmly, "I see you take me for an absolute fool. I have come this far, beaten you twice and don't intend to follow you only to live a life of mediocrity."

The Sarkany continued in a hypnotic tone, "I see you don't really understand. Let's talk. Elias, you probably don't know this, but the castle from which your ancestors come from was once hallowed ground for the Aba Clan. A Hungarian, King Károly, and his troops took their fortress by force, and for many years the Hungarian people of the surrounding villages, like the one where you and your family now live, served this castle like slaves, whether they liked it or not."

"Interesting history lesson, but…"

"Oh, that's not the end of the story. To protect this fortress, those who hid themselves in these very walls decided to build a gun tower in the lower castle. But it was useless. Do you know *why* it was useless?"

Impatient and irritable, Elias said, "I'm sure you're eager to tell me."

"It was useless because your ancestors were cowards. The guards surrendered the castle to the Turks without as much as a scuffle."

The Sarkany reached for his own neck with both hands, pulled the amulet up to his face and slipped it over his head. He placed it on a rock before Elias and sat back.

"They did absolutely nothing. Does that sound familiar?" Without waiting for Elias to respond, he continued. "More than a hundred years later, it was recaptured for Hungary. You, I am sure, come from this cowardly lineage."

Dismissing his taunt, Elias responded, "You

said yourself that it was taken back by the rightful owners, didn't you?" Elias asked. "The amulet does not belong to you."

The Sarkany leaned forward to rattle Elias. He picked up the amulet and held it in the palm of his hand. He looked at it and kissed it before returning it to the boulder near the fire.

"It truly looks like it is mine," the Sarkany said.

"Not for long."

"You *really* think you can reclaim this amulet?"

"As you said, why else would I seek you out?" Elias asked.

"Well, Elias, you don't have to fight me for it. I was planning to give it back to you if we could come to some kind of mutual agreement," said the Sarkany.

"I don't believe a word you say. Anyway, I want nothing given to me by the likes of you. I am prepared to draw my sword and complete the job."

"You know, Elias, when you fight me, you are fighting yourself," the Sarkany said in a slow and even tone.

"That's where you're wrong. You may look like me, but you are nothing like me. You are but a foul boil attached to my soul, and you are ready to be lanced. You are about self-loathing, deception, and empty-heartedness," said Elias.

"You may be right, but follow my ways and don't subject yourself to what might be or who you might become. Elias, my dear friend, be ordinary and content. Ordak will be proud that you decided to follow me—to him. You will go home, putting this misguided adventure behind you, and live a life full of others' hopes and wishes. Your papa will embrace you."

Shattered and weary, Elias felt he was under a slow, draining spell. His muscles lost their tension, and he began to think about his relationship with his father. He didn't like how he felt so detached from him. Elias yearned for his affection and wanted the same proud smile that Papa offered his brother Kristof.

It was working. The Sarkany saw that his evil ways finally struck a chord with Elias. Now, the Sarkany knew just the right chink in Elias' armor to attack. He continued.

"Make your papa proud. Go back home and tell him you want to work by his side on the farm. It's not so bad. Most everyone you know does it. They are happy. Don't they seem to be happy, Elias? Don't *you* *want* to be happy? If not, you may become something that you end up despising—someone *others* despise. Don't you despise me?"

"Are you telling me that if I follow you, Papa will love me more?"

"He wants you to give up your foolish dream. He has told you that your path will lead to heartache."

"He *did* tell me that." Elias dropped his sword, sat on a boulder, and stared into the fire.

"Yes! Yes, he did! What else did he tell you?"

"He said I was selfish to pursue my talents and that I should learn a trade."

Star slowly took steps, inching his way closer to Elias.

"Don't you want to be a good son? He's getting old and needs more help on his farm."

The fire between Elias and the Sarkany roared stronger, and its heat was even more intense. The amulet glowed and shimmered in the light of the fire. The Sarkany stood motionless, waiting for Elias to make the next move or respond to him.

In the cool air, Elias sat encased in confusion.

Pricked by a thousand pinpoints, he felt the sweat drip from every pore. His mouth was dry. What seemed like horrifying flashes of lightning ricocheted in his head and it cluttered his thoughts. Star got louder with each whinny.

"Shut up, you ugly beast!" The Sarkany screamed, drowning out Star. "Tell me, Elias! Tell me more about Papa."

With every breath the Sarkany took, the fire leapt with demonic dancing flames. The crackling blaze reached new heights, and expanded its boundaries. Star whinnied more and more. He drowned out the Sarkany. Star punctuated each syllable uttered from the Sarkany. Like the slap of rough ocean waves on a beach, Star continued to whinny and whicker, and as the sounds intensified, Elias began to disengage himself from the hold that the Sarkany had on him.

"Elias, I said, tell me more. What else? Tell me more secrets that lie in your heart. You must know secrets. Tell me your *deepest* secrets."

Secrets, Elias thought. *What secrets do I know?* Elias mumbled, "You must know how close and how long…"

"What are you saying?" the Sarkany asked.

"…to expose it to what could destroy it…feel it…don't think it…how close and how long to expose it to what could destroy it…feel it…don't think it."

"What are you babbling about?"

Regaining his composure, Elias stood and looked directly at his mirror image.

"You asked me what secrets I knew. Little did you know what a stupid move you just made. STUPID, but thanks anyway."

Elias reached for his sword. The Sarkany grabbed the amulet from where it was perched.

"So you want to fight me for this piece of meaningless jewelry?"

"Think what you will. I already have the amulet," Elias shouted.

"Oh? What's this then?"

Elias took his left hand, the one holding the sword, and raised the hilt to his chest and rested it gently and squarely there, just as Lantos showed him.

"Believe me when I tell you that I have seized the amulet," Elias insisted.

"Then you won't need this any longer," said the

Sarkany.

The Sarkany heaved it with all his might down into the roaring fire and, with that, the inferno gained more intensity.

"If you want it, you know where it will be—melting," said the Sarkany.

"You're an arrogant fool. All I want from you is your head. So you may have heard—third time's a charm."

"Ah … you are bold and brash and just like me," said the Sarkany.

The Sarkany pulled his sword from the sheath and advanced toward Elias while taking wild slices into the air. Close enough to land a blow, Elias raised his sword swinging it with a vengeance. As the metal collided onto its twin sword with a *ping*, he heard the once small, faint voice inside him grow louder. With each bang of steel on steel, as Zoltan foretold, the voice became more distinct within him. He, however, still couldn't understand its message. *What does this mean?* Elias thought.

Fighting gallantly through his fatigue, Elias, however, was losing ground to his adversary. The

Sarkany forced him backward as Elias protected himself from the wild yet fierce blows of his archenemy. Every slice through the smoky air ended with the reverberating *CLANG! CLANG! CLANG!* of steel. Sparks flew. The Sarkany got the upper hand and relentlessly pushed Elias closer and closer to the rage of the fire. With little time to spare, he heard the voice within remind him—*the Sarkany cannot kill me but will allow me to destroy myself.*

"No way am I going to be the victim of my own false move," Elias shouted.

His own reassurance was all he needed. His adrenaline rushed, and he lunged at the Sarkany. His action forced the Sarkany in a spot between Elias and the raging flames. Frantically spinning around, the Sarkany swiped but missed him with the blade, but the knuckle guard of the sword's hilt landed on the inside of Elias' wrist.

"AHH—ow! You piece of scum!" Elias, screamed in agony, and dropped the sword. He doubled over while holding his wrist. As he did, the Sarkany, with some relish advanced—only to find that Elias had swooped up his sword with his right hand. Elias held him at bay with an outstretched arm. The Sarkany retreated a few paces to plan his next advance.

As if a new world opened to him, the voice in Elias' head was now clear. He heard *exsisto verus ut vestri—be true to yourself*. He heard *exsisto unus per pectus pectoris—be one with the heart*. Over and over, the voice inside of him repeated the phrase, *exsisto verus ut vestri—be true to yourself…*

The battle waged on as sparks flew with the clash of the twin blades. Both swordsmen thwarted every advance of the other. Turning and thrusting, the force of each blow was beginning to lose its power and velocity. *Ping, ping, ping!*

The Sarkany, seeing the results of Elias' exhaustion, began to back him closer to the jagged cliff. Step by step, the Sarkany was goading Elias to make a false move and plummet a hundred feet onto the unforgiving boulders below. Elias felt the ominous edge only a few paces behind him.

Confusing the Sarkany and throwing him off guard, Elias tossed his sword to one side and out of his reach. The Sarkany smirked and said, "So you are ready to join me."

"You read that move the way I wanted you to—no. Don't count on it," he replied.

Confused, the Sarkany dropped his guard. Before he pulled his thoughts together, with lightning speed, Elias reached down and whipped out the dagger from his boot with his ailing left hand. He lunged toward the Sarkany and plowed the dagger's long blade into the middle of his chest.

The sheer thrust of the motion forced the Sarkany to drop his sword and he staggered back on his heels. He let out a gruesome groan, and fell back to the ground. He was sprawled lifeless on his back within a foot of the fire.

Elias, dripping with sweat, dazed and weak, stood and picked up his sword. He walked to where the Sarkany lay and stood over him. Looking down at him, Elias assumed he was dead but the strength of the fire grew and flames shot upward while Star, again, began to whinny. Elias, not knowing what to think, froze where he stood. The wind came from the east and stirred the ash, sand and debris in a vicious whirl. The voice in his head was now crystal clear as he heard, *exsisto verus ut vestri—be true to yourself … exsisto unus per pectus pectoris—*

be one with the heart, over and over again

When the cutting wind died down, The Sarkany stood in front of him. Their eyes met icy and clear.

"Elias, the voice you once heard within you was mine, but it was yours as well. The voice you now hear is yours and only yours. You have defeated your worst fear."

"I was told never to believe a serpent. Why should I believe you now?" Elias asked.

"You should not trust me. You should trust yourself. You have found your voice. Although it comes from within, others will hear it when you approach them. The day you decide to cast away the truth of your heart, you may see me again. In fact, I'll be looking for you. I understand that you think I may be telling you a lie, but nothing of value in life comes easily. I know this, as I was once alive. Yes, I am your enemy, as I was in my other incarnations, but that is my nature, and it is something I cannot escape. As I am defeated today, I tell you to believe what you will. Just as you believe in yourself, your worst enemies believe in themselves."

The Sarkany turned around and walked into the

fire. When he did so, it raged in force but within seconds, it died down to the size of the original campfire that Elias had built hours earlier. It was gone. There was no sign of the Sarkany as if it completely burned up in the fire.

Weak and exhausted, Elias saw the amulet intact in the smoldering embers and he used his sword to rake it out. He was pleased at the sight.

He pulled out a blanket from the saddlebag and lay next to the burning embers. Weary, he could barely keep his eyes open. As his sight blurred, his eyelids opened and closed. In his fog, he could make out Star standing next to him. His eyes tired, he again closed them. Moments later, he opened them again but Star was gone. He thought he saw Zoltan walking from the campsite. He fell asleep and slept throughout the rest of the day and into the night.

*****

Elias awoke to a wet, coarse tongue licking his face. "Cimbora, it's you, boy! How did you get here? Does Zoltan know you followed me?" Elias was delighted to see his old friend, and as he lay back with Cimbora kissing his face, he saw the Turul in the sky.

251

"This is going to be an awesome day. But where were you guys last night?"

He saw a small pouch attached to Cimbora's collar. He looked in it and found a note from Zoltan.

Elias,

I hope you will take good care of Cimbora. I am happy that you believe in yourself, but always remember those who believed in you.

Zoltan

Elias jumped to his feet and looked in all directions for Star but he was gone. He found his sword thrust into the earth with the amulet lying on top of the hilt. He reached for the amulet and examined it, front and back. Gratified as he held in the palm of his hand, he pulled a thin leather strap from the saddlebag. He tied it to the amulet and slipped it over his head.

He collected the two swords, and he walked to the arch where he had found the first sword at the onset of his journey. He pulled back the stone, placed them both into the compartment, and covered the entrance. He made sure his sketchbook was safe.

TWENTY-TWO
Elias' Journey Begins Anew

I t was the end of the day—the very day when many who lived close to the hamlet ventured to the village square. Here, the villagers and rural folks would purchase, sell, trade staples and socialize. Most times there would be a juggler or clown both competing for attention. Musicians with stringed instruments of all kinds filled the air with a variety of sounds.

Mr. Varga, owner of the apothecary shop, swept his stoop. He peered over the wall to see only one of the usual three old men sitting outside the tavern. He sat alone and drank a mug of beer. He tried to grab the attention of strangers to wield his disparaging points of view. Like water and vinegar, he did not mix well, regardless of how much he tried to shake up the conversation. The other "ugly men," as Nattymama had called them, had recently become ill with excruciating headaches.

The villagers, who included the hunched-over

man who sold trinkets, jewelry and odd little statues, and the woman who peddled blankets and other items she had stitched, as well as the butchers and farmers who sold meats, eggs, and vegetables, were weary from a long day. They began to pack up their stations and prepare to return to the comfort of their own homes.

Mama was alone, as usual, in the kitchen, chopping fresh vegetables and small cubes of meat as she prepared the evening meal. She hummed a song of her own. The rich aroma of her bubbling sauces wafted in and out of their modest home and delicately bounced on a mellow breeze. She would often pause and tear up as she worried about Elias. She kept her thoughts and her prayers to herself. She had to be strong, as her family depended on her. She knew in her heart that he was safe.

Dripping with sweat, Kristof worked the field where the fledging stalks of summer wheat were thriving. Proud of his work, it was time to call it a day. He called for his brother, Jozef, to join him for a swig of water before their short hike home for supper.

As she did most days, Nattymama tended to her garden and walked to her spot to rest. She sat on the stone bench near the stream. This was her favorite spot to rest and reflect on important matters. She enjoyed hearing the water bubbling and gushing over the smooth flat stones that did little to impede its flow. Thinking that nature is predictable and knowing that life has a way of improving itself, she sat and inhaled all that nature offered her.

"Nattymama!"

She heard her name in the distance but paid it no attention. She recognized the voice and the corner of her mouth turned up.

"Nattymama! Where are you?"

She remained silent because she knew that Elias would find her where he always found her at this time of day.

Elias, barely containing his joy, sprinted up and sat beside her. As if she were meditating, she kept her gaze focused on the stream. Elias looked to the water and smiled. She turned, reached to him with open arms, buried her face in his chest, and cried.

"Happy birthday, Elias. Happy birthday."

"Happy birthday? I've been gone a long time, but I didn't realize it had been that long."

"You have made an old woman very happy."

"What do you mean? We haven't seen each other. We haven't…"

"Hush, my Elias. I know. I see it in your eyes. I feel it in your presence. You must go to see Papa."

"Yes, you're right, but I don't know what he will think of me."

"Just go. Trust me. You will find him where you go and paint. He goes there every day. His heart is broken and he thinks you will never come home. He has this tiny ounce of hope that today will be different. Just go. There will be more time for Nattymama and Elias. GO!"

*****

The day that Elias returned, the sky was a deep blue with only a veil of clouds on the horizon that floated above the smooth and rolling mountain crests. The heavens were now a smear of the day and the rays of the sun were soft and blended with the green hills.

Perched high upon the cliff where Elias would come to paint, Papa sat alone. Never before in his long life did he appreciate the natural beauty of the Hungarian landscape as he did now. It was as if he were seeing it for the first time. "This must be what my boy—my young man—knew from a young age," Papa said, talking to the heavens. "Why was I so blind?"

From a hundred paces away, Elias shouted, "Papa, Papa, I've come home!"

Papa stood and spread his arms. He landed in his father's arms nearly knocking him over. Papa patted the back of Elias' head with his large, calloused hands.

"I thought you would never come home. I thought…I thought…"

"It's okay. I'm here now, Papa. I came home."

"Look at me," Papa placed his big hands on either side of Elias' face and looked into his eyes, "I haven't looked at you since you were a little boy…a little boy. I have missed so much as you have grown up right before me, but I did not see it. It has been like magic."

"Oh Papa, you've seen me."

"Listen to me. I realized something—it's miraculous when a person stops and thinks and feels the beat of their own heart," Papa said.

Elias said nothing but gave him a reassuring smile.

"I am proud of you, son. What you did was courageous. It wasn't long after you left that I came to grips that my words were reckless and hateful. It was not long before I understood that I had mistreated you, but I knew you and thought I lost you forever. I don't deserve a boy like you."

"Please Papa…"

"My Elias, I want you to have something."

Papa reached down and picked up something that was next to where he had been sitting. He handed Elias a long and slender package covered with crumpled brown paper.

"Go ahead. Please, unwrap it."

Elias cautiously tore the paper and found the most beautiful object within. He delicately removed the wrapping, and as he did, a tear ran down his face. It was a paintbrush, and its delicate handle was laced in gold.

"This is beyond words. I am the happiest son in the world."

"I am the happiest Papa. You came back"

"But, of course, Papa. I always come home."

"I traveled to the next village over and found it. A tall older man with a long white beard was peddling his wares in the town square. I told him I was looking for you. As if he didn't hear what I said, he reached down, pulled out a box, and in it was this brush. He told me he could not take my money and said he trusted me to place it in the hand of someone who is deserving. He said that a deserving person would appear to me soon. I asked for the box to keep it safe and when I did, he said nothing and walked into a tent with the box in hand. He must have gone out the back as I never saw him again. But enough of that. I must tell you, son, of my adventure of getting there and home. That can wait."

"Papa, I will tell you about my journey as well."

"My dear Elias, your journey is only about to begin."

About the Author

E.G. Kardos grew up loving fantasy. Art of all kinds has played an important role in his life as long as he can remember. He's written several books both for readers who are young and young at heart. Inspiration for what he writes comes from the beauty that surrounds all of us—both in nature and in each other.

Connect with the author at: **www.edwardgkardos.com**
Look for E.G. Kardos on Face Book, Twitter and other social media.

*****

73603184R00148

Made in the USA
Columbia, SC
14 July 2017